House
on
Haunted Hill

ISBN: 979-8-9886823-1-8 (hardback)
          979-8-9886823-0-1 (paperback)

Printed in the United States of America

House on Haunted Hill

Resurrection

GARY J. ROSE

OTHER BOOKS BY THE AUTHOR

Jeannie Loomis Thriller Novels
(In order of release)

Ark of the Covenant-Raid on the Church of Our Lady Mary of Zion
(ISBN: 978-0-9988777-3-0)

Was there really an Ark of the Covenant containing the original stone tablets of the 10 Commandments written by God? If so, where is it presently located? Nancy, a biblical historian believes she knows the location but enlists the help of her boyfriend, Frank, and his elite band of rogue ex-military special forces team. Together they formulate a precise plan to steal the Ark from its location in Ethiopia. Already suspicious of the criminal activity of the Banshees, the FBI and Interpol are watching their every move.

Star Chamber
(ISBN: 978-0-9988777-7-8)

"No man is above the law and no man is below it: nor do we ask any man's permission when we ask him to obey it." Theodore Roosevelt. FBI agent Jeannie Loomis is back and needs closure after the disastrous ending to the Ark of the Covenant investigation. The Star Chamber, a secret tribunal, is in session, judging individuals in absentia for acts against the United States. This judicial body tries individuals above the law due to their political power, wealth, or celebrity status. A guilty verdict results in a death sentence carried out by the equally secret SDL group. One of the first to receive a death sentence is a former secretary of state. As the death toll rises, Agent Loomis and her team stumbled into the workings of the secret court while investigating child pornography, sex trafficking, and a mysterious "sex island."

Forgotten Plans
(ISBN: 978-1-7348524-1-7)

As the holiday season approaches. FBI Special Agent in Charge, Jeannie Loomis and her team are investigating a possible robbery of a Bank of America branch in San Francisco by decorated Vietnam War veterans trained as tunnel rats. As that investigation is developing, the Department of Homeland Security (DHS) and the National Security Agency (NSA) have found information on a thumb drive collected during the raid on Osama bin Laden's compound in Pakistan which issues future fatwas in the event of his death.

Three teams of jihadists arrive in the United States to carry out the deceased al Qaeda leader's orders. Loomis, racing against time, must decide what events scheduled in the San Francisco Bay Area would meet the criteria of being worthy targets. Will Loomis and her team have enough time to prevent another 9-11?

House of Special Purpose
(ISBN: 978-1-7348524-8-6)

House of Special Purpose, was the Bolshevik code name for the Ipatiev House, used as a place of confinement for the last czar of Russia, Nicholas II, and his family, after his forced abdication of the throne. After spending seventy-eight days in the house, during the early morning hours of April 17th, 1918, the royal family is escorted to a basement room where they were assassinated. The killing squad was shocked and horrified when the bullets from their weapons bounced off the czar's children. Unbeknownst to them, the royal jewels of the Romanoff dynasty had been sewn into their undergarments. Finding the jewelry, the secret police, Cheka, confiscated the property and place it in a vault, only to discover items missing during an audit in 1925. While special agent Jeannie Loomis and her partner, Ismail Flores, attend Super Bowl LIV in Florida, Ricky Pinheiro, Jeannie's love interest, attends a high-level briefing at the NSA where he is informed that the possible location of the missing Romanoff jewelry are in the hands of a Russia oligarch living in San Francisco. He is using the jewelry as collateral to fund left-wing anarchy. In Dallas, the FBI is closing in on a lone wolf jihadist desiring another 9-11 type attack on the United States. Before his capture, he flees to the underbelly of the Haight-Ashberry district in San Francisco and becomes the focus of Loomis and her team.

Time Game
(ISBN: 978-1-7348524-3-1)

In Time Game, his fifth Loomis novel, Special Agent Loomis and her team are investigating the death of three guards killed in an armored car robbery containing $25 million dollars bound for an Indian casino hosting a poker championship. Jeannie, however, has been requested by the Marin County Sheriff's Department to assume the role of task force manager in pursuit of a vicious serial killer who preys of women using his charm and seduction. As Jeannie attempts to bring the serial killer to justice, not only does the body count rise but Joey, the former leader of the assassin group (Sons and Daughters of Liberty) who carried out verdicts for the clandestine Star Chamber Court resurfaces. The mastermind that led to the killing of her fiancé hints at a massive attack against those that he feels are undermining the culture of American society. The Time Game has started.

Thin Blue Line
(ISBN: 978-1-7348524-4-8)

Someone is making a game out of killing cops in the San Francisco bay area. With a city already out of control due to liberal politics, the citizens, including law enforcement, are on high alert knowing a serial killer is among them. When one of Loomis's own FBI agents is killed, the FBI is requested to take over the investigation. As Jeannie and her team search for the bay area killer, she is requested by the San Jose Police Department who has their own cannibalistic killer on the loose.

The Fourth Reich
(ISBN: 978-1-734852-4-7-9)

"The Fourth Reich" is an electrifying indie thriller featuring the captivating and flawed FBI Agent Jeannie Loomis as its fierce female lead. In this gripping story, Jeannie finds herself entangled in a treacherous web of genetic manipulation, international intrigue, and the resurgence of Nazi ideology. On an uncharted island off the coast of Argentina, Dr. Wolfgang Hausser, a descendant of the infamous Auschwitz doctor Joseph Mengele, has been conducting heinous experiments in eugenics. Driven by his desire to resurrect the Fourth Reich, Hausser has embarked on a mission to clone Adolf Hitler himself using the Fuhrer's DNA, which he has obtained from the Russian secret police, FSB.

Black Cell/Black Heart
(ISBN: 978-1-7378736-2-4)

FBI agent Jeannie Loomis, a flawed but dedicated agent, who believes that sometimes the ends justify the means, is attempting to remain below the radar with the corrupt administration at the top of the bureau. While on a much-deserved vacation with her boyfriend, Interpol agent Sean Delaney, she is contacted by the Idaho State Police asking for a consult regarding a recently found body dump-the result of an active serial killer. Delaney is called away after the broadcasting of the Super Bowl was hacked by a group calling themselves, the Black Cell. Black Cell's goal is to bring the superpowers of the world to the brink of nuclear war, but is that their ultimate goal?

The Phantom Train
(ISBN: 978-1-7378736-5-5)

A double homicide of a mother (niece of a former SS officer) and daughter, leads a strong female FBI agent who believes the ends justify the means, to a hidden diary of a former Waffen SS death camp guard who hid one of Hitler's phantom gold trains. With the aid of Mossad, the two agencies try to locate the train while modern-day Nazis attempt to get there first.

This is the ninth Jeannie Loomis thriller novel. The novel is historically based and relevant to current searches being done by treasure hunters in Europe.

Warning: There are chapters dealing with the various Nazi death camps.

Rollercoaster
(ISBN: 978-1-7378736-7-9)

Rollercoaster is an exhilarating indie thriller/adventure introducing the reader to the return of the captivating and determined FBI agent Jeannie Loomis. In this heart-pounding story, Jeannie finds herself in a race against time alongside her team and the A.T.F. (Bureau of Alcohol, Tobacco, Firearms, and Explosives) after a devastating act of terrorism strikes a fictional amusement park in California.

Non-Fiction Books

Hitting Rock Bottom (Amazon best-seller)
(ISBN: 978-0-9988777-0-9)

They came from many of the high schools, middle schools, and continuation schools of Placer County due to truancy, multiple suspension, expulsion, probation referrals, or court order. Most hated school and school authority. Several had lengthy criminal histories already and some were from rival gangs. Forty-two males and females would start wearing Army camouflage versus street clothes. They would undergo the hardest academic and physical rigor of their lives. Most met the challenge - some did not. This was their last chance of avoiding dropping out of school, living a life of crime, incarceration, or death. There they would run into a retired police sergeant who would be their teacher. He prided himself on being "old school" and with the help of the U.S. Army, they together, help transform these youth into high school graduates and productive adults. They were inspired by books/ films such as Freedom Writers, Stand and Deliver, To Sir With Love, Gridiron Gang and Dangerous Minds to the point of wanting to share their stories with others. For most "cadets" the academy became their family. Through their writings, the reader will enter the lives they had been living before attending the academy. They explain how they began noticing changes in both their attitude, physical fitness, and family life. It was their dream that at least one at-risk student would become inspired by their book and decide, after Hitting Rock Bottom, to turn their lives around like they did.

Towards the Integration of Police Psychology Techniques to Combat Juvenile Delinquency in K-12 Classrooms.
(ISBN: 978-1-4935569-5-3)

Dealing with student's behavioral problems is one of the most pressing concerns facing educators today and teachers are feeling inadequately equipped to meet the challenge. The objective of this book is to better understand prevailing delinquency problems in K-12 classrooms, and how teachers address them. Although calls to improve school safety and discipline procedures have escalated, teachers do not have all the tools needed to achieve the goal. This book determines the components of police psychology, and the socio-ecological model that might logically be included in a program designed to reduce k-12 classroom delinquency, based on current theory and research. In this model program, highly trained law enforcement officers who are knowledgeable in the art of interacting with behaviorally and emotionally troubled individuals in real-life scenarios, like those faced by educators in classrooms, would train pre-service teachers to handle challenging behavioral situations; thus, reducing the amount of delinquency in classrooms.

How to Create a Public-School Military Style Boot-Camp Academy for Troubled Teens (A Blueprint)
(ISBN: 978-0-9988777-2-3)

This book describes how a public school district or office of education, can create, and run a successful military-style boot camp academy for "at-risk" students, based on how the author created that Alder Grove Academy in Auburn, Ca. It lists a blueprint from formulation to running the program.

Teaching Inside the Walls
(ISBN:978-0-9988777-6-1)

What is it like teaching in a juvenile detention facility, county jail or state prison environment? Get used to massive security checks, doors opening and closing electronically and being escorted by correctional officers. There will be the constant clanging of bars, catcalling by inmates, prisoners being escorted to various locations in the facility and the occasional assaultive inmate who requires more than one correctional officer to escort.

Welcome to the work of an "at-risk" teacher of incarcerated juveniles and adults.

How do you teach these individuals in these types of environments? This "how-to" book gives you the answers.

DEDICATION

From the depths of my childhood, an unforgettable moment unfolded as I witnessed the premiere of the legendary horror masterpiece, House on Haunted Hill, forever immortalized by the mesmerizing performance of the late Vincent Price. At a tender age of ten, the sheer terror that coursed through me during this cinematic experience surpassed anything I had ever encountered before.

As the years went by, my mind often wandered into the realm of possibilities for a sequel, envisioning the chilling trajectory of this haunting tale, not to be confused with the other films using the same title. Thus, the seed of an idea blossomed, and it gave life to the script and novel for House on Haunted Hill: Resurrection, a contemporary continuation of the nightmare.

Drawing inspiration from the original film's haunting legacy, our story unfolds with the emergence of our protagonist, freed after serving a grueling 20-year prison sentence for the murder of his wife,

Annabelle, within the dreaded House on Haunted Hill itself.

Throughout his trial and subsequent confinement, Frederick Loren endured the scornful mockery of self-proclaimed psychics. The cruelty inflicted upon him stoked the fires of revenge that burned within his soul, propelling him to orchestrate a nightmarish haunted house party akin to the premise of the initial film.

Each guest, including those who once derided him, would be lured by the irresistible offer of $100,000 – a substantial reward for those who survive a single night in the infamous House on Haunted Hill. This mansion, situated in the ethereal embrace of Southern California's Ennis House, stands as the very location where the original film first breathed life.

House on Haunted Hill: Resurrection dares to resurrect the primordial terror, beckoning readers on an unrelenting odyssey of psychological torment, suspense, and vengeance. Frederick Loren, having acquired the house from Watson Pritchard, the sole survivor of the first night's horrors, gathers a motley crew of guests for the macabre affair. Among them are an attorney grappling with a crippling alcohol and gambling problem, Loren's loyal personal secretary, a retired homicide investigator, a secretary from one of Loren's many businesses, and three self-proclaimed psychics – individuals whom Loren seeks to expose as fraudulent in the face of true supernatural forces.

As the doors lock, sealing everyone within the foreboding mansion, the malevolence woven into its very fabric awakens. This house, originally constructed in Spain for the First Inquisitor Torquemada, carries the weight of its dark history. The spirits of Torquemada and others, long confined within its walls during its abandonment for over two decades, now yearn for restless retribution.

Prepare to be spellbound as the haunting legacy unfurls once more, leaving in its wake lingering questions of the supernatural, justice, and the deepest recesses of human nature. House on Haunted Hill: Resurrection beckons you to embrace terror anew, venturing into a realm where the boundaries of the mortal and the ethereal intertwine, daring you to confront the demons that reside within.

Original movie poster 1959

BACKGROUND

There it sits atop the hill, a haunting reminder of
its former glory. Located in the hills overlooking
Southern California, the foreboding mansion stands
tall against the night sky. Tonight, like most nights, it
is engulfed in a thick layer of fog adding to its mystery
and dread. The wind howls, whispers emanate from
broken windows and cracked walls, and a rusted iron
front gate creaks and groans. Weeds and thorny vines
have taken over the once formal gardens.

In the year 1959, an eerie and bone-chilling incident
unfolded within the walls of this infamous residence,
a place that seemed tailor-made for a haunted house
party. And it was precisely this macabre idea that
Frederick Loren embraced to celebrate his wife's
birthday. Little did he know that the night would be
fraught with horrors beyond his darkest imaginings.

Their marital union could hardly be described as
blissful. Frederick harbored a deep-seated belief that
his wife, Annabelle, had once attempted to poison
him. The suspicion weighed heavily on his mind,

driving a wedge between them. When he confronted her about it, Annabelle merely scoffed and dismissed his concerns, attributing his illness to nothing more than a bout of food poisoning.

However, beneath the facade of their strained relationship, there existed a far more sinister undercurrent. Secrets lingered in the shadows, casting doubt and suspicion on the true nature of their connection. The echoes of whispered accusations reverberated through the halls, mingling with the chilling winds that swept through the old house.

As Annabelle's birthday approached, she reluctantly agreed to host a haunted house party, eagerly anticipating the presence of her dear friends. Yet, as the guest list materialized, a startling revelation emerged—none of her companions had received an invitation. The realization struck her like a thunderbolt, leaving her feeling isolated and betrayed. What had initially appeared as a gesture of love now appeared to be a calculated move by Frederick to further fuel their turbulent relationship.

Unbeknownst to Annabelle, Frederick had sinister intentions hidden beneath his charming facade. The haunted house party he orchestrated was not merely a whimsical affair; it was a wicked tapestry of deceit and terror, designed to push the boundaries of their fractured bond to the edge of madness. With every flickering candle and every creaking floorboard, the ominous atmosphere heightened, drawing them both deeper into a twisted game of trust and betrayal.

Frederick Loren extended a peculiar invitation to five individuals, beckoning them to spend a fateful night within the notorious House on Haunted Hill. The lure was irresistible: if they could endure the night's terrors and emerge unscathed, each would be rewarded with the handsome sum of $10,000. Although by today's standards it may not be a significant fortune, in the year 1959, when the average annual income stood at a modest $5,600, such a windfall held the promise of a life-changing opportunity.

The eclectic group of invitees comprised individuals from diverse backgrounds, each driven by their unique motivations to accept the tantalizing proposition. Among them was a daring test pilot, whose insatiable thirst for thrills led him to embrace the challenge without hesitation. A troubled reporter burdened by an addiction to alcohol and a mounting gambling debt also found solace in the allure of this enigmatic venture.

Another participant, a secretary working within one of Loren's sprawling business ventures, eagerly embraced the invitation as she sought desperately to alleviate the weight of her mounting debts. Her financial struggles became an irresistible pull toward the promise of a brighter future.

The owner of the house itself, a Mr. Watson Pritchard, chose to attend despite being haunted by a harrowing past experience. Having spent a night in the very same house, he emerged with his sanity barely intact, convinced beyond doubt of its paranormal nature. His own brother had met a grisly demise within those bloodstained walls, his body gruesomely dismembered, with the exception of his severed head which was never found. Pritchard, too, found himself in dire need of financial assistance, his desperation compelling him to set foot once more into the heart of darkness.

As the clock ticked closer to the appointed hour, these disparate souls prepared to embark on a shared journey, their paths interwoven by fate's unyielding hand. Unbeknownst to them, the House on Haunted Hill held secrets that would test their mettle, unravel their deepest fears, and lay bare the truth behind their tangled destinies.

Once the guests had gathered within the eerie confines of the mansion, Frederick Loren took center stage, introducing himself and setting forth the unyielding ground rules that would govern their night of terror. The stakes were high—each participant must remain within the haunted House on Haunted Hill until the morning light, enduring the spectral terrors that awaited them, all in pursuit of the coveted $10,000 prize. As the servants departed, the mansion descended into an oppressive silence, devoid of electricity and illuminated solely by the flickering glow of gas-fed lamps.

Locking the doors with impenetrable steel and securing the windows with forbidding bars, the guests found themselves sealed within a labyrinth of darkness. It was the perfect recipe for a Halloween haunted house party—just add a handful of ghosts, and the stage was set for a night of spine-chilling horror.

Among the peculiar assembly, a lingering sense of suspicion shrouded Frederick Loren's thoughts as he extended an invitation to a psychiatrist. Doubts gnawed at his mind, hinting at concealed motives hidden beneath the doctor's seemingly benign facade. What secrets lay veiled behind those penetrating eyes? Only the treacherous journey through the House on Haunted Hill would lay bare the true intentions of this enigmatic figure.

As the hands of the clock drew nearer to the appointed hour, these disparate souls steeled themselves for the unimaginable. Their paths intertwined by the relentless grip of fate; they embarked on a shared odyssey into the heart of darkness. Unbeknownst to them, the House on Haunted Hill held more than just ghostly apparitions—it clutched tightly onto long-buried secrets, capable of unraveling their deepest fears and exposing the twisted tapestry of their intertwined destinies.

Would they emerge triumphant over the spectral forces that lurked within? Or would they succumb to the relentless embrace of the encroaching darkness, forever entangled in the malevolent grip of the House on Haunted Hill? Their ultimate fates, and the hidden depths of their own souls, could only be revealed as the night unfolded its sinister dance.

Amidst the gripping aura of suspense, the haunting memory of a past tragedy weighed heavily upon the gathering. The tale of Mr. Watson Pritchard's own brother, brutally murdered within these very walls, resonated as a chilling reminder of the horrors that awaited. The macabre details unfolded—the dismembered remains, each body part discovered except for the missing heads. Pritchard, himself barely clinging to life when he was discovered, also sought solace in the promise of financial relief that this night held.

And so, with the inclusion of the psychiatrist and the haunting specter of Mr. Pritchard's past, the group stood on the precipice of an enigmatic journey, one that would push them to their limits, test their resolve, and expose the true nature of their beings.

Now that you, the reader, grasp the perilous circumstances thrust upon the ill-fated guests in the year 1959, an inevitable question arises—what transpired on that fateful and horrifying night? From the moment the guests crossed the threshold, chaos ensued, setting the stage for a nightmarish ordeal.

As the guests stepped foot into the foreboding mansion, an ominous sign manifested immediately—a colossal chandelier descended from above, narrowly missing one of their trembling figures. The air crackled with an unsettling energy, foretelling the malevolence that lurked within those haunted halls. If this harrowing incident wasn't enough to instill terror, fate conspired against them further.

The servants, entrusted with the keys to their escape, inexplicably departed before their designated time, severing any possibility of an early exit. Those who harbored the desperate desire to flee were now ensnared within the clutches of the mammoth estate, its formidable walls serving as both a prison and a breeding ground for restless spirits.

Within the mansion's depths, the ethereal entities stirred, their presence growing increasingly restless. Whispers echoed through the corridors, spectral apparitions materialized and dissipated in the blink of an eye, and an otherworldly chill permeated the very air they breathed. The forces that had long haunted the House on Haunted Hill reveled in their newfound audience, eager to unleash their supernatural wrath upon the unfortunate souls trapped within.

The guests, confronted with an escalating torrent of supernatural phenomena, would soon face the ultimate test of their resilience and courage. The veil between the living and the dead grew thinner with each passing moment, blurring the boundaries of reality and nightmares. Their survival, both physical and spiritual, hung precariously in the balance, as the mansion's secrets unfurled and the vengeful spirits sought to claim their unwitting victims.

To further complicate the already dire situation, Frederick Loren harbored a delusion that the House on Haunted Hill could be transformed into a mere playground of Halloween pranks. Blinded by his skepticism, he believed that the spirits lurking within its walls were nothing more than figments of imagination. Little did he realize, until it was too late, that the ghosts that resided within the house were not amused by petty tricks and contrivances. Their wrath needed no embellishment, for it was the authentic essence of their tormented souls.

Adding a twisted layer to the unfolding tale, there existed a hidden motive behind Loren's invitation to the psychiatrist. Unbeknownst to the others, his true intention was to expose the illicit affair that had taken root between himself and Annabelle. The specter of infidelity cast a dark shadow over their relationship, a secret that Loren could no longer bear to conceal. By luring the doctor into the clutches of the House on Haunted Hill, he sought to unearth the affair and expose it to the world.

In a chilling turn of events, the doctor met a grisly end within the bowels of the cellar. Murdered by Loren's own hands, his lifeless body was mercilessly disposed of in a vat of acid—a sinister act that only served to satiate the malevolent energy craved by the spirits that haunted the house.

Yet, Frederick Loren's macabre journey was far from over. Fate conspired to present him with a sinister twist. Annabelle, driven by her own curiosity and concern for her lover, descended the stairs to the cellar, unaware of the deadly fate that awaited her. Manipulating a skeletal apparition, Frederick plunged her into a state of paralyzing fear. In her panic, she stumbled and met a horrifying demise as her body dissolved into the corrosive depths of the acid.

Satisfied with the grim outcome, Frederick Loren relinquished himself to the clutches of the authorities. After his conviction, he was sentenced to spend the next four decades behind prison walls, paying the price for his heinous deeds. And it is at this juncture, with the haunting events of the past firmly cemented, that our story truly begins to unfold.

CHAPTER 1

1979 – The House on Haunted Hill

THE NIGHT HAD taken a turn for the worse, transforming into a dismal scene. The House on Haunted Hill was shrouded in an eerie fog that permeated its surroundings, while a chilling rain began to descend. Seeking refuge from the elements, old Sam, a weathered homeless veteran, found solace in the presence of an overhang near a side entrance of the house. Slowly, he trudged up the driveway, pushing his grocery cart loaded with all his worldly possessions, passing the deteriorated iron gate that had long lost its ability to secure the parking area.

With meticulous care, Sam unloaded his meager belongings and gingerly spread out his worn bedroll on the ground, strategically situating it as close to the door as he could. In his state of destitution, he sought solace wherever he could find it. His weathered hands rummaged through his scant possessions until they stumbled upon a bottle of inexpensive liquor. A glimmer of hope flickered within him as he clung to the belief that this modest indulgence would offer a brief reprieve from the harsh bite of the cold.

As he raised the bottle to his lips, the disheveled state of his beard, once vibrant, now showcased an almost complete transformation into shades of gray. The passage of time had etched its mark upon him, a visible testament to the hardships he had endured.

An Army veteran, experienced the harsh reality of societal marginalization, where he felt discarded and forgotten. Despite his initial appreciation for his service, the support he received was limited to access to a VA clinic, leaving him with a sense of disregard for his dedication to his country. Although he managed to resist falling into the clutches of drug addiction, he sought solace in occasional refuge in alcohol. His modest grocery cart became a source of comfort, accompanied by the sporadic nourishment of church-provided meals and the meager means to purchase a fresh bottle of spirits.

Wearing his worn-out U.S. Army veteran baseball hat, Sam would sometimes panhandle near grocery stores, hoping to earn a few extra dollars alongside the occasional "Thank you for serving" accolades. He assumed that those who offered him donations were aware that he would spend the money on his chosen vice—liquor. Another day, another dollar—a fleeting thought that unknowingly became one of his final contemplations before his tragic demise.

Settling onto his bedroll, Sam took another swig from his inexpensive bottle of liquor. Oblivious to his surroundings, he remained unaware of the slow, quiet opening of the door behind him. Suddenly, without warning, an eerie sensation gripped him as a ghastly, elongated hand emerged through his back, piercing through his chest. Sam's mind struggled to comprehend the grotesque sight of an arm protruding from his own body, while blood oozed from his open mouth. Before he could even react, the spectral arm enveloped his lifeless figure, forcefully dragging him into the depths of the haunted house. With an ominous slam, the door sealed shut, forever trapping him within the sinister confines of its walls.

As the echoes of the slamming door faded, an eerie stillness settled upon the scene. Astonishingly, the blood and remnants of Sam's gruesome demise mysteriously vanished, absorbed into the house, leaving no trace behind. Only the bottle of booze draining its last drop, abandoned bedroll, and grocery cart, stood as witnesses to the inexplicable events that had unfolded.

San Quentin Prison

1979 – Release Day for Frederick Loren

In the quaint city of San Quentin, nestled adjacent to the notorious San Quentin Prison, life carried on with its usual rhythm. Sometimes referred to as San Quentin Village or Point San Quentin Village, it was a modest enclave that lacked the grandeur of a bustling metropolis. A collection of merely 40 single-family houses and a small condominium complex with ten units formed the entirety of this close-knit community. Its population, a mere 100 individuals, lent an air of familiarity and intimacy to the place.

On this particular day, San Quentin basked in the ambiance of tranquility with a slight twist. The gentle breeze from the nearby San Francisco Bay swept through the streets, whispering its secrets to anyone willing to listen. The waves, as they lazily caressed the shoreline, lacked the ferocity that often accompanied them, as if their impact had been softened by the serene atmosphere that enveloped the village.

The main difference today in the unassuming city of San Quentin, was the palpable sense of excitement and anticipation hanging in the air. The serene streets were disrupted by the sudden arrival of numerous television vans, their towering satellite dishes reaching towards the sky. Today marked an extraordinary occasion—the impending release of Frederick Loren, a man infamous for the chilling murder of his wife within the notorious House on Haunted Hill.

News crews from far and wide had descended upon San Quentin, eager to capture every moment of this high-profile event. Cameras were poised, journalists ready to report, as the small city braced itself for the spectacle that would unfold. The past crimes and haunted history surrounding Frederick Loren had captured the imagination of the public, turning this community into the center of attention.

San Quentin, typically known for its tranquility and modesty, now found itself thrust into the spotlight, its streets abuzz with a mixture of curiosity, morbid fascination, and a hint of apprehension. As the countdown to Frederick Loren's release commenced, the city held its collective breath, awaiting the next chapter in this chilling tale.

Sally Farnsworth, once a prominent figure in the world of journalism, had experienced a tumultuous fall from grace. Once gracing the screens as a prime-time television newscaster, she now found herself relegated to the role of a street crime reporter.

Whispers and rumors circulated about the reasons behind her sudden downfall. Some speculated that an ill-fated affair with a high-ranking executive had led to her undoing, as allegations of a potential sexual harassment suit emerged. When confronted with the salacious evidence of explicit text messages and compromising photos exchanged with her lover,

Sally's resolve wavered, and she recanted her threats. Nevertheless, the damage to her career had already been dealt.

Capturing the story of Frederick Loren's emergence from behind the ominous prison walls could serve as her much-needed catalyst for redemption. She had been there, reporting on the original murders back in 1959 that had captivated the nation's attention. Now, she envisioned herself at the forefront of a compelling television special—a platform where she could retell the chilling tale of that fateful night, casting a spotlight on the horrors that unfolded within the House on Haunted Hill.

This special would be her ultimate chance to prove her worth, showcasing her journalistic skills and ability to captivate an audience. With each passing moment, her determination grew stronger, fueled by a deep-rooted desire to resurrect her reputation and reclaim her rightful place in the media world.

CHAPTER 2

AS SHE STOOD in that moment, a sense of recognition washed over Sally when she noticed a familiar face making his way towards her. It was Jim Hammer, a rising star among reporters from a rival network. His arrival added an extra layer of tension to the already charged atmosphere. Towering at an impressive height of 6'2", he possessed a striking handsomeness that was accentuated by his recent teeth-whitening procedure. Hammer was undoubtedly on the fast track to promotion, racing ahead in his career with great speed.

"So, today's the day Frederick Loren gets released, huh?" Jim remarked, breaking the silence between them. Sally nodded, a mix of disbelief and cynicism tinging her response. "It's hard to fathom that he only served twenty years of his forty-year sentence, especially considering his wealth. I suppose money doesn't always guarantee leniency in the justice system. Rumor has it his investments have tripled during his time behind bars, turning him into a multi-billionaire."

Jim let out a low whistle, his voice tinged with a touch of incredulity. "Well, that's something. Kills his wife, spends two decades as a millionaire behind bars, and emerges a billionaire. Life can be ironic. But now he's plagued with a failing heart and needs a walker just to move around."

As Jim Hammer and Sally Farnsworth engaged in conversation, their rivalry momentarily set aside, a touch of wistfulness colored their exchange. "If I had his money, I'd escape to my own private island, surrounded by servants who'd attend to my every need," Sally remarked, her voice tinged with a hint of envy. The allure of such extravagant wealth was undeniable.

Jim nodded, a flicker of uncertainty crossing his face. "There have been rumblings around the office. It seems there might be some changes on the horizon. The coveted 6 pm slot would indeed be a step up. I'll throw my hat in the ring, but there's stiff competition. Plenty of kiss-asses working overtime to secure that spot. We'll have to wait and see what happens."

Their conversation soon veered towards the very story that had brought them to this moment—the case of Frederick Loren and the House on Haunted Hill. Jim, eager to gather insights from Sally's firsthand experience, inquired about the details. "You covered the original case, right? What can you tell me about it? I've only heard fragments, like him killing his wife and something about ghosts haunting the house," he said, a hint of laughter in his voice, quickly interrupted by a fit of coughing induced by his cigarette.

Sally paused, reflecting on the dark history that had captivated the nation. "Yes, I was there from the beginning. The story is more chilling than just a murder. It was a night of terror, an evening where guests were lured to the House on Haunted Hill with the promise of riches. But what awaited them within those walls was a living nightmare. Unexplained phenomena, ghostly apparitions, and a sense of evil permeated every corner. Frederick Loren's wife was indeed killed, but there's so much more to the story. It's a tale that still sends shivers down my spine."

As their conversation unfolded, a shared understanding emerged between them. The stakes were high, not only in covering the release of Frederick Loren but also in their personal aspirations within the competitive world of journalism.

The exchange between the two reporters underscored the complex nature of Frederick Loren's story. It was a tale of wealth, crime, and the elusive nature of justice. The anticipation of his release stirred a mix of fascination and contempt within the media, as they prepared to chronicle the rise and fall of a man who seemed to defy conventional expectations at every turn. Loren's life could catapult their careers to new heights.

With their rivalry simmering just beneath the surface, Sally and Jim acknowledged the significance of the moment unfolding before them. Their paths were destined to intersect, their competition serving as a catalyst for capturing the truth behind Loren's transformation from convicted killer to wealthy magnate. As the minutes ticked away, they both understood that the story of Frederick Loren's release held the potential to shape their futures in ways they had yet to comprehend.

"You know, back when it happened, the case was almost as notorious as the Charles Manson saga," Sally began, her voice carrying a mix of fascination and intrigue. As they delved deeper into the details of Frederick Loren's life, a complex picture started to emerge.

"He was a man of means, with numerous businesses and properties to his name," Sally continued. "But his marriages were far from successful. Annabelle, the wife he ultimately killed, was his fourth spouse. There was quite an age gap between them, and it's been speculated that she may have been motivated by his wealth when she married him. Nevertheless, their relationship took a dark turn."

Jim leaned in, curious to uncover the intricacies of the story. "So, what exactly happened?"

Sally took a sip from her coffee cup, savoring the moment before continuing. "Well, for Annabelle's birthday, Frederick came up with a rather macabre idea. He decided to host a haunted house party, inviting a group of people who were complete strangers to him and his wife. And to entice them, he promised a staggering $10,000 each if they could spend a night in the supposedly haunted house."

Jim raised an eyebrow, intrigued by the audacity of the proposition. "How many people actually took him up on that offer?"

Sally paused, a hint of a smile playing at her lips. "Believe it or not, quite a few brave—or perhaps desperate—souls accepted the challenge. Despite the rumors and the ominous reputation of the house, five people were drawn in by the promise of a hefty sum. Little did they know what awaited them within those haunted walls."

As the conversation unfolded, Sally and Jim embarked on a journey into the chilling depths of the House on Haunted Hill. The story that lay before them was a maze of mystery, greed, adultery, and the insatiable human desire for wealth and adventure. With each passing moment, the anticipation grew, setting the stage for the retelling of a night that would forever be etched in the annals of infamy.

As the wind off the bay rustled through Sally's hair, she took a moment to collect her thoughts. Recounting the guests who had accepted Frederick Loren's chilling invitation, she painted a picture of an eclectic group entangled in a web of intrigue.

"Like I mentioned, there were five brave souls who dared to spend the night at the House on Haunted Hill," Sally began, her voice carrying a hint of excitement. "If memory serves me right, one of them was a newspaper columnist, seeking a story that would captivate readers. Another was a daring test pilot, drawn to the adrenaline of the unknown."

Sally paused, her eyes scanning the horizon as she tried to recall the remaining individuals. "There was also a psychiatrist, who tragically met his end within those haunted walls," she continued, a touch of somberness in her tone. "But the most curious guests were the secretary and a fifth person that for the life of me, I can't remember. Oh well, it will come to me. The two reporters observed the side prison door believing there was activity, but it was a false alarm. "So, what exactly transpired in the house that night?"

The words lingered in the air as Sally's gaze turned inward, her mind wrestling with a missing piece of the puzzle. A quiet moment passed before a spark of recollection flickered in her eyes. "Ah, yes. The fifth person," she whispered, piecing together the fragments of memory. "The owner of the house, once host to the very horrors that awaited the ill-fated guests. He now resides in a mental institution, forever marked by the events that transpired."

With each revelation, the House on Haunted Hill grew more enigmatic, its history intertwined with the lives of those who had stepped into its haunting embrace. Sally's journalistic instincts sharpened, recognizing that within this tale of terror lay the potential to unravel secrets and expose the depths of the human psyche. As the winds continued to whip through the air, Sally couldn't help but wonder what mysteries would be unearthed as she ventured deeper into the heart of this haunting tale.

As the conversation delved deeper into the twisted dynamics of Frederick Loren's ill-fated marriage, Sally revealed a startling truth that lay at the heart of the story.

CHAPTER 3

"LOREN HAD HIS suspicions," Sally began, her voice tinged with a mix of intrigue and apprehension. "He believed that his wife, Annabelle, had made several unsuccessful attempts to poison him. The desire for a divorce was burning within him, but Annabelle adamantly refused to grant him that freedom."

Jim, perplexed by the situation, questioned why Loren didn't simply file for a divorce. Sally's response carried a touch of historical context. "Times were different back then, Jim. Divorce wasn't as readily accessible as it is today. Loren found himself trapped in a marriage that had turned toxic, with no straightforward means of escape."

Sally continued, her voice carrying a sense of foreboding. "In a bid to both celebrate Annabelle's birthday and orchestrate an eerie twist of fate, Loren planned a haunted house party. Initially, Annabelle agreed, under the assumption that her friends would be in attendance. However, when she discovered the true nature of the event, she vehemently refused to participate."

Jim was captivated by the unfolding narrative. "So how did Loren manage to make her attend against her will?"

A somber pause enveloped the air as Sally chose her words carefully. "That's when things took a truly sinister turn. Loren, in a display of cunning and manipulation, somehow forced Annabelle to attend the haunted house party. It was at that moment, when the boundaries between reality and terror blurred, that the story truly started to unravel."

As Sally's words hung in the air, the gravity of the situation became all too apparent. The haunted house party was not merely a whimsical celebration; it was a stage for a sinister game of control and revenge. The events that were about to unfold would forever shape the lives of those involved, and as Sally and Jim continued their conversation, they couldn't help but feel a chill creeping up their spines.

As Sally continued to wrestle with her wind-blown hair, the conversation shifted towards the infamous haunted house itself, nestled high in the foothills overlooking Los Angeles. Her voice carried a blend of fascination and unease as she shared her knowledge.

"The alleged haunted house is a sight to behold," Sally began, her eyes distant as if envisioning the ominous structure. "Designed by some famous architect, it possesses an exterior that befits its reputation. Some would say it looks like a damn haunted house, with its imposing presence and mysterious aura. It is located all by itself high up in the foothills overlooking Los Angeles."

Jim, intrigued by the descriptions, confessed that he had never seen the house firsthand. "I've heard rumors about the windows and doors, though. Are they as formidable as they say?"

Sally's nod was accompanied by a somber expression. "Indeed, in the course of the trial, it was uncovered that numerous previous owners had undertaken significant renovations, fortifying the house extensively. The windows had been fitted with bars, effectively obstructing any potential means of escape, while the doors were constructed with solid steel. This deliberate transformation fostered an aura of confinement and seclusion within the eerie confines of those walls. Curiously, the trial failed to disclose the motive behind such elaborate measures, whether they were intended to deter outsiders or to confine individuals within once they set foot inside."

Her words carried weight as she continued, painting a vivid picture of the house's state. "Loren purposely left the house in a state of disrepair and neglect. Cobwebs and dust adorned the interior, remnants of years of dormancy. And as the guests arrived, he had set up Halloween pranks, adding an extra layer of eerie anticipation."

Sally leaned closer, her voice dropping to a hushed tone. "The first prank to unfold was a falling chandelier that narrowly missed one of the guests. It set the stage for the tension and fear that would pervade the group throughout the night."

Jim listened intently, his curiosity growing. "So, what happened next? How did Loren guide them through this haunting ordeal?"

Sally's voice carried a mix of macabre fascination and disbelief. "Loren welcomed the guests into the haunted house, gathering them together to lay down the rules. To claim the $10,000 prize, they had to survive the night within the confines of the house. He emphasized that once locked inside, the steel doors could not be opened until morning. The windows, barred and impassable, only added to the sense of entrapment. And with Pritchard, the house's owner, attesting to its haunted nature, it was a chilling cocktail of fear and anticipation."

As Jim digested the unsettling information surrounding Pritchard and the gruesome events that unfolded within the haunted house, he couldn't help but express his incredulity. "Pritchard sounds like a man on the edge of sanity. Surviving a night in the house, witnessing the deaths of his brother and others... Why would he subject himself to such horror again?"

Sally sighed, her voice tinged with a mixture of empathy and curiosity. "Who knows, and you're right, Jim. Pritchard's belief in the haunted nature of the house bordered on obsession. He claimed to have barely escaped with his life during that fateful night, where his brother and six others perished in inexplicable circumstances. And to make matters even more chilling, he asserted that while body parts of his brother were found, his head was never recovered."

Jim shook his head in disbelief, his eyes reflecting the horrors of the tale. "Jesus, that's beyond disturbing. Pritchard certainly seems like someone who belongs in a mental institution. Is he still alive?"

Sally nodded, her voice laden with a hint of sadness. "Yes, Pritchard is still alive, but his mind remains trapped in the labyrinth of his traumatic experiences. Following that night when Frederick Loren committed the brutal murders of his wife and her lover, the doctor, Pritchard's mental state deteriorated to such an extent that it's uncertain if he will ever find his way out of the confines of the state mental hospital."

Jim's mind was reeling with the revelations, yet he couldn't resist delving further into the darkness. "During the trial, it was disclosed that Loren disposed of the bodies by immersing them in a vat of acid, previously used by a previous owner experimenting with wine blends. Is that true?"

Sally's voice lowered, mirroring the gravity of the revelation. "Yes, the trial brought to light the macabre details of Loren's actions. After committing the heinous murders, he callously discarded the bodies in a vat of acid, repurposing it from its original wine-related use. It was a chilling testament to the depths of Loren's depravity."

As their conversation reached its climax, a sense of unease loomed over them. The mysterious activity by the prison doors seemed to amplify the tension in the air. Sally and Jim knew that they were on the brink of unearthing a story that would challenge their perceptions of fear, deceit, and the unknown. The House on Haunted Hill held dark secrets, and they were determined to expose them to the world, regardless of the risks involved.

CHAPTER 4

THE SIDE DOOR of the prison swung open, revealing a correctional officer stepping out onto the grounds. Following closely behind, aided by a walker, was the infamous Frederick Loren. Despite the effects of time and a slight stoop in his posture, Loren's imposing figure still commanded attention. Standing tall at 6'2", he possessed a distinguished aura accentuated by his full head of gray hair and a neatly trimmed mustache. Dressed in a dark blue suit and a tasteful tie, he exuded an air of refinement that contrasted with his dark past.

Accompanying Loren was another correctional officer, carrying his personal belongings. As they made their way towards a waiting limousine, a chauffeur stood ready, opening the rear door in anticipation of their arrival. With careful precision, the guards handed over Loren's belongings to the waiting driver, ensuring that nothing was amiss.

Sally and Jim observed the scene, their journalistic instincts heightened by the sight of the man whose name had become synonymous with the horrors of the House on Haunted Hill. This was their moment, the beginning of an arduous journey to unravel the secrets that lay dormant within the enigmatic figure of Frederick Loren. Little did they know the extent of the darkness that awaited them as they embarked on their pursuit of truth.

Sally mustered up the courage to confront Frederick Loren, her voice steady as she posed her first question. "Mr. Loren, how does it feel to be released from prison after two decades?" However, her inquiry was met with a chilling silence as Loren remained unresponsive. Undeterred, she pressed on, determined to extract some semblance of emotion from the enigmatic figure before her. "Do you feel any remorse for killing your wife?"

Loren slowly lifted his head, his piercing gaze fixated on Sally and the other reporters gathered around. A sinister smirk played on his lips as he raised an eyebrow in a gesture that sent shivers down Sally's spine. Without uttering a word, he turned his attention to the awaiting chauffeur, who assisted him into the waiting car. The vehicle swiftly departed the parking lot, leaving behind a lingering sense of unease.

Sally turned to Jim, her voice tinged with a mix of trepidation and curiosity. "That grin of his... It sent chills down my spine. Do you think we'll hear from him again?"

Jim nodded, fully aware of the influence Loren's vast wealth held. "With his resources, we can expect his presence to make waves once more." They knew that their encounter with Loren was just the beginning, and the mysteries surrounding him were far from being laid to rest.

CHAPTER 5

THE FOLLOWING MORNING, within the confines of his opulent library, Frederick Loren sat comfortably in an executive high-back leather chair alone. The room exuded an air of antiquated grandeur, adorned with dark oak wall coverings, shelves lined with leather-bound books, and exquisite antique furniture. The warm glow of a Tiffany bank desk lamp illuminated the expanse of his oversized desk, upon which files were meticulously spread out.

Loren's focused attention was abruptly interrupted by a sharp knock on the door, momentarily snapping him out of his contemplation. Intrigued by the unexpected visitor, he beckoned them to enter, his mind buzzing with the possibilities that lay ahead. Little did he know that this encounter would set in motion a series of events that would further intertwine his fate with the House on Haunted Hill and the insidious forces that lurked within its walls.

"Good morning, Mr. Loren," Stacey began, her voice filled with genuine concern. "How did you sleep? It must have been a relief to be back in the comfort of your own bed."

Loren, still adjusting to the newfound freedom and the reality of his release, offered a faint smile in response. "Indeed, Stacey. There's nothing quite like the familiarity of one's own sanctuary. It feels good to be home. Why do you call me Mr. Loren? You have been my personal secretary forever, yet since I've been home, you don't call me Frederick."

"Sorry Mr. Loren, I mean Frederick, you have been gone for so long and when I talk to people on your behalf, I always say, Mr. Loren. I'll do better, I promise."

She was a woman in her early fifties and possessed an air of intelligence and confidence that radiated from within. Her dedication to maintaining a healthy lifestyle was evident in her toned physique, a testament to her unwavering commitment to fitness. Her dark shoulder-length hair, neatly pulled back into a ponytail, gave her an ageless appearance, resembling someone in their late thirties or forties.

As Loren gazed upon Stacey, he couldn't help but appreciate her unwavering loyalty and the invaluable support she had provided over the years. She was not just his secretary; she was his confidante, his trusted advisor, and the one person who truly understood the complexities of his mind.

"I appreciate your presence, Stacey," Loren acknowledged, his voice carrying a mix of gratitude and admiration. "Your unwavering dedication has been an essential pillar of my life. Please continue to assist me as we embark on this new chapter."

Stacey nodded, her eyes reflecting a deep understanding of the magnitude of the journey that lay ahead. With their unique bond and shared history, they both knew that their intertwined destinies were far from reaching their conclusion. Together they would navigate the treacherous waters of wealth, power, and the ominous legacy that surrounded the House on Haunted Hill. Little did they know that their reunion would mark the beginning of a harrowing tale, filled with dark secrets, eerie encounters, and a battle against forces that defied the realms of the living and the dead.

Stacey placed the carafe of coffee on Frederick Loren's desk, her eyes drifting to the scattered files that lay before him. Curiosity piqued; she couldn't resist inquiring about the individuals selected for the upcoming venture.

"So, you've chosen a select few from the pool of those intrigued by your haunted house invitations?" Stacey inquired; her voice laced with genuine interest.

Loren looked up from the files, a mischievous grin playing upon his lips. "Indeed, my dear Stacey. I have carefully selected a group that encompasses a variety of backgrounds and motivations. Among them are individuals in genuine need of financial assistance, as well as three self-proclaimed psychics who have, quite frankly, irked me with their fraudulent claims during my trial and subsequent television appearances. It's time to expose their true nature to the world."

He picked up the first file, labeled "John Hawthorne," and opened it, revealing the information within. Stacey accepted the file, her eyes scanning the contents with interest. "John Hawthorne, a retired and highly decorated homicide detective. A thrill-seeker, it seems, though I suspect there may be more to his motivations," she mused, noting his handsome features captured in the photograph.

Loren's eyes sparkled with amusement as he observed Stacey's reaction. "Ah, yes. John Hawthorne possesses a certain charm, doesn't he? Quite the devilish allure. Now, let's discuss Jeannie Manning, a successful attorney perpetually seeking new challenges. The promised $100,000 will serve as a means for her to settle her substantial gambling debts. A pretty face, wouldn't you say?"

Stacey's gaze shifted to the file labeled "Jeannie Manning," her interest aroused. She perused the details, taking note of Jeannie's accomplishments and the debts that weighed upon her. "Yes, she is indeed a striking woman," Stacey acknowledged, a glimmer of intrigue in her eyes.

"Next, we have Sarah Owens," Loren began, his voice filled with empathy. "A young nurse struggling to make ends meet while caring for her elderly mother, who suffers from Alzheimer's. On top of that, she bears the burden of an outstanding student loan. I hope she possesses the strength to endure the night."

Stacey nodded, acknowledging the hardships Sarah faced. She understood the weight of financial struggles and the challenges of caring for a loved one with a debilitating condition. Their hearts went out to her, recognizing the importance of her presence in this unfolding tale.

Loren paused, setting his coffee cup aside, before delving into the next phase of his plan. "Now, let's address the psychics," he declared, pulling out three additional files from his desk drawer. He opened the first one, revealing Rachel Henry's name and story. "Rachel Henry claims to possess a heightened sensitivity to psychic phenomena and energy. She insists that she can tap into subtle signals and gather information from the beyond. We shall soon discover the truth of her claims."

He opens the next file. "Jonathan Riley is commonly referred to as an empath due to his heightened sensitivity towards the emotions and energies of others. He possesses the ability to perceive and comprehend the feelings of individuals around him. However, there are doubts about his authenticity." He passes the file over to Stacey.

"And lastly, we have Madame Redzepova, a highly regarded spiritualist," Loren presents a stack of articles to Stacey. "These clippings highlight her expertise in various practices, including seances and tarot card readings. Madame Redzepova firmly believes in the existence of spirits, the afterlife, and actively engages in communication with the spiritual realm. She claims to possess the ability to communicate with the deceased. I wonder if she will be able to establish contact with Annabelle once we enter the House on Haunted Hill." Loren hands the final two files to Stacey and stretches, letting out a yawn.

"Can I ask you a question about all this?" Loren leans forward but does not answer.

"I understand your desire to expose these psychics as charlatans, but why is it so important to you? Is it because of what they put you through during the trial and how they constantly belittled you on television?"

"It goes beyond what they did to me during the trial, but that is a part of it. They played a significant role in manipulating the public's perception of me. These frauds prey on people's fears and vulnerabilities, claiming supernatural abilities while making a mockery of the justice system. It's crucial to expose their deceit for the sake of truth and justice. They manipulate and exploit the innocent, offering false hope and taking advantage of their vulnerability. By revealing their true nature, we can protect others from falling victim to their deceptive practices and ensure justice prevails."

Stacey dismissively shakes her head, displaying a hint of skepticism. "Well, it's their money. If individuals choose to bestow their hard-earned funds upon these swindlers, so be it. I recall watching documentaries about ministers who claimed to miraculously eliminate cancerous growths from people, employing a deceptive approach of operating on these supposed victims without anesthesia and then removing animal organs, the 'cancerous growth'. It always amused me how easily some individuals could be deceived, but once again, if they willingly choose to part with their money due to their own naivety, let them face the consequences."

Loren disagrees, emphasizing the importance of exposing the truth. "No, I don't see it that way. I have an opportunity to unmask them and protect the vulnerable from their harmful antics. It's not just about seeking retribution for the personal attacks against me; it's about safeguarding others from their fraudulent claims and ensuring justice is served."

Stacey sighs and concedes, "Well, it's your money. I think you've done enough for today. Why don't you take a nap?" she suggests. "While you are sleeping, I will prepare the invitations. All we need is a final date."

"The funny thing is, I'm not tired. I just wish the construction crew would hurry up and finish the house so we can set a final date for the party. Have you heard from him?" Loren asks, shifting the conversation.

"Yes, I just spoke to him on the phone before I brought you coffee. The construction foreman informed me that the house is nearly ready. He mentioned that it could benefit from a thorough cleaning, as it has accumulated cobwebs and dust over the years of disuse. If you'd like, he can arrange for a cleanup crew to come in. Additionally, he would like to know if you can visit the house in the next few days, so he can demonstrate how everything operates."

"Call him back and let him know we don't need a cleaning crew. The dust and cobwebs contribute to the haunted house ambiance. I'll arrange to meet him the day after tomorrow, preferably in the morning. It's all coming together, just as I planned." Loren concludes, eagerly anticipating the progress of his haunted house party in the House on Haunted Hill.

CHAPTER 6

STEVE WARNER HAD dedicated more than three
decades of his life to the construction industry, always
with the goal of eventually retiring. The opportunity
to renovate the infamous mansion, often referred to as
the House on Haunted Hill, seemed like the perfect
steppingstone towards that dream. When he received
a phone call from Frederick Loren's personal secretary,
outlining an extensive list of tasks to be completed on
the house, along with the promise of an unlimited
budget, Steve knew it could significantly contribute
to his retirement plans.

As the sun began its descent, Steve decided it was
best not to risk any injuries or potential worker's
compensation complaints. He promptly called his
crew, informing them that they should wrap up their
work for the day and resume the following morning.

"Alright, everyone, let's call it a day," Steve declared.
"It's getting dark, and given the limited lighting
inside this place, I don't want anyone to get hurt." He
scanned the surroundings, his gaze falling upon the

absence of Frank, one of his notoriously unreliable workers.

Steve's frustration echoed through his muttering as he questioned the whereabouts of Frank. "Where the hell is Frank?" he grumbled, his patience wearing thin. "Damn it! If he's drinking on the job again, I swear I'll fire him."

Suddenly, an eerie wind swept through the area, causing a nearby door to slam shut with a loud bang. The unexpected noise startled everyone in the vicinity, their attention drawn to the mysterious occurrence. As if in response to the supernatural moment, the same door began to creak open slowly, revealing an empty space behind it.

With a mixture of curiosity and caution, Steve cautiously approached the door. To his surprise, out stumbled Frank, who appeared surprisingly sober for once.

"Where the hell have you been? We're about to wrap up. Did you complete the bathroom I assigned to you?" Steve's frustration seeped through his words.

"Damn boss, you scared the crap out of me slamming that door," Frank replied, visibly shaken. The rest of the construction crew exchanged confused glances, still recovering from the eerie encounter.

Steve himself was still a bit unsettled by the earlier door incident. "Did you manage to install all the hidden cameras?" he asked, trying to regain his composure.

"Yeah, the bathroom's done, and all the cameras are in place," Frank responded. "The computer monitors are set up behind the hidden wall in the cellar. They just need their batteries charged since, you know, there's no electricity down there."

"Alright, I'll remind the owner. He's scheduled to visit in two days," Steve replied, his thoughts lingering on the unsettling atmosphere of the place.

"I'm telling you, boss, this place gives me the creeps. It felt like I was being watched the whole time I was working here," a shaken Frank replied.

"Agreed. Let's get out of here. We should be done by tomorrow." With a shared sense of unease, the crew prepared to leave the premises, eager to put the eerie experiences of the House on Haunted Hill behind them.

A week had passed, and the much-anticipated date of the haunted house party at the House on Haunted Hill had finally arrived. From an upstairs window of the mansion, Frederick Loren observed the scene unfolding before him. Six sleek black limousines ascended the hill, their headlights piercing through the darkness, illuminating the narrow and winding road that led to the ominous summit. Leading them was a funeral hearse. A nice touch, Frederick thought. The atmosphere was cloaked in an eerie ambiance as anticipation hung in the air. The large recently repair iron gate opened at their advance.

The procession of black limousines came to a halt just outside the imposing mansion. As the car doors opened, the guests began to step out, one by one. John Hawthorne, a retired homicide investigator known for his sharp mind and athletic build, was the first to exit his limousine. Standing at 6'0" with dark hair and dressed casually, he adjusted his jacket and surveyed the grandeur of the mansion before him, his eyes scanning its imposing presence. A quick pat reassured him that his 9mm was secured in its shoulder holster.

Following closely behind, the second limousine unveiled Ms. Jeannie Manning, an attorney at law. With an attractive appearance and long, cascading dark hair, she possessed an air of elegance. Ms. Manning gracefully followed Hawthorne up the driveway into the mansion's courtyard, intrigued by the enigmatic atmosphere that surrounded them. An aria of suspense lingered in the air, as if the house itself held secrets waiting to be unveiled.

From the third limousine, the driver stepped out and assisted Watson Pritchard, a man of eccentric demeanor and haunted appearance, to exit the vehicle. Watson's eyes darted nervously, absorbing the foreboding presence of the mansion's façade. With a firm grip on a small bag, he clung to it tightly, seeking solace in its contents. He was all too aware of the lurking terror within the depths of the House on Haunted Hill, carrying the weight of its secrets deep within his troubled soul.

Among the arrivals, Ms. Sarah Owens stood out as a young and attractive woman who could easily be mistaken for a college student. Though shorter in stature compared to Ms. Manning, she shared the same cascading long dark hair. As she glanced at the formidable mansion, a look of fear danced across her features. Pulling her small suitcase from the backseat of the limousine, she cautiously followed in the footsteps of the three individuals who had preceded her, apprehension evident in her every step.

Following closely behind, Jonathan Riley arrived at the scene. With an average height and a slender build, he sported a distinguished mustache that added a touch of character to his appearance. A mischievous smile played upon his lips as he joined the path to the mansion.

Ms. Rachel Henry, a slender woman with short blonde hair, embodied a bookish demeanor as she approached. Clad in a dark blue business suit, she regarded the house with an indifferent expression on her face. Following Jonathan Riley's lead, she pulled her small suitcase along, maintaining an air of mystery around her. As a psychic with an innate connection to the supernatural, she exuded confidence, her gaze fixed upon the house as if she could discern the energies lingering within its walls.

Finally, from the last limousine, Madame Redzepova emerged from the backseat with graceful ease. In her late sixties, she carried herself with an air of wisdom and mystery. Adorning her neck were several strands of jewelry, and her attire resembled that of a gypsy, with a flowing dress that exuded vibrant colors.

As she cast her eyes upon the house, a smile played upon her lips, reflecting a mixture of anticipation and excitement. However, there was also a subtle hint of nervousness that flickered in her expression, betraying the weight of the unknown that lay ahead.

Perched in his elevated position, Frederick Loren smiled contentedly. All six guests had finally arrived, completing the group for the haunted house party. Additionally, Stacey, his secretary, had already settled into her room within the house. The stage was set, and the anticipation swirled in the air.

A playful grin danced across Loren's face as he voiced his thoughts aloud, knowing full well that no one was present to hear him. "I wonder what the ghosts have planned for us tonight?" he mused, embracing the thrill of the unknown that awaited them within the House on Haunted Hill.

CHAPTER 7

As all seven individuals reached the imposing front door, it swung open on its own accord, eliciting a collective gaze of uncertainty among the group. With a sense of trepidation, they cautiously stepped inside, their eyes darting from one another to the darkened corners of the entrance hall. Watson Pritchard, in particular, exhibited heightened unease.

Silently, the group advanced into a spacious hallway, their footsteps echoing softly against the ancient floorboards covered by what was once very expensive tapestry rugs, now worn thin due to age. At the end of the hallway, they entered a grand room, its atmosphere heavy with a mysterious allure. Suspended from the center of the ceiling, a large chandelier hung, adorned with thirteen gas-fed lamps that emitted a dim illumination, casting eerie shadows across the room. The ambiance was hauntingly captivating, filling the space with an aura of both intrigue and caution.

"Did you notice that the chandelier has thirteen lights?" Hawthorne inquired, making his way toward Sarah Owens, his curiosity evident.

She smiled, a touch of unease lingering beneath the surface. "No, I didn't. This place already gives me the creeps. Hi, I'm Sarah."

Hawthorne extended his hand in greeting. "I'm John. Do you happen to know Mr. Loren?"

"Nice to meet you, John. No, I don't. And you?" Sarah replied, returning the handshake.

"No, I haven't had the pleasure. Though I've heard about him—the trial, his wealth, and all—but never actually met the man," Hawthorne explained. As he absentmindedly brushed his hand against a bookcase, a cloud of dust filled the air, revealing neglected cobwebs scattered throughout the room. "Well, he certainly has created the perfect atmosphere for a haunted house party," he commented, observing the eerie ambiance that surrounded them.

As the main entrance door slammed shut with a resounding echo, Sarah instinctively screamed, seeking solace in the comforting presence of Hawthorne. The chandelier above them swayed back and forth, stirred by the sudden gust of the closing door. Sarah glanced up at Hawthorne, a tinge of embarrassment coloring her expression. "I'm so sorry. I'm just freaking out for some reason."

Jeannie Manning approached Sarah, retrieving a prescription bottle from her purse. "This might help calm your nerves. It's Valium," she offered, concern etched on her face.

Sarah politely declined, shaking her head. "No, thank you. It's just a case of nerves and lack of sleep. I'll be alright," she assured Jeannie. With a shrug of her shoulders, Manning walked away, leaving Sarah to collect herself.

At the top of the stairs, Frederick Loren and Stacey observed the interaction between the guests. "Good evening," Loren greeted, slowly descending the stairs with the assistance of his walker. Stacey followed closely behind. Once he reached the final step, he grasped his walker firmly, directing his attention back to the assembled guests.

"I'm Frederick Loren," his tone warm and welcoming. This is my personal secretary, Stacey. I want to express my gratitude to all of you for accepting my invitation to the haunted house party here in the House on Haunted Hill." His eyes caught sight of the swaying chandelier. "It seems the ghosts are extending their own welcome to you all as well."

"Mr. Loren, you, of all people, know better than to mock the spirits within this house. They are already restless this evening," Pritchard cautioned, his grip on the duffle bag tightening, as if finding solace in its presence.

Loren's expression shifted, a subtle hint of a sarcastic smile playing on his lips. "Perhaps you have a point, Mr. Pritchard," he responded, his voice laced with amusement. "Shall we make our way to the dining room? I imagine you must be famished. Feel free to leave your belongings here; we'll retrieve them later when I show you all to your respective rooms."

With a sense of uneasiness, Pritchard reluctantly joined the group, still clutching his bag protectively to his chest, unwilling to part with it. Together, they proceeded towards the dining room, the air thick with anticipation.

An enticing spread of food awaited them on the expansive dining room table, accompanied by meticulously arranged place settings for each guest. The group took their seats, with Loren and Stacey positioned at the head of the table. Jeannie Manning, unable to resist the allure, promptly helped herself to a glass of wine. Pritchard, mirroring her actions, followed suit.

Two elderly servants, dressed in black and white uniforms, stood stoically against a wall, their expressions unreadable as they observed the gathering of guests.

Loren paused, acknowledging the tension that had settled among the guests. He raised his glass of wine, and the others followed suit. "Here's to food, drink, and perhaps a few ghosts," he proposed, a mischievous glimmer in his eyes. Before Pritchard could voice his objection, Loren caught the implication of his remark. "Oh, my apologies, Mr. Pritchard. I seem to have done it again, haven't I?"

Pritchard glared at Loren, frustration evident on his face, before pouring himself another glass of wine. As the dinner drew to a close, Loren rose from his seat and addressed the group, his commanding presence filling the room. Silence enveloped the gathering as all eyes focused on him.

"The rules are simple yet challenging. If you can endure one night in this haunted house, each of you will be rewarded with a generous sum of $100,000," Loren declared, his voice firm. "There is no electricity within these walls. The gas-fed lights, casting their eerie glow, serve as our only illumination. I believe the atmospheric lighting, accompanied by the dust and cobwebs, add to the overall ambiance, don't you agree?" Not waiting for an answer, he continued. "There is no phone service, and any attempt at communication with the outside world would prove futile. Once the servants depart, the house will be securely locked, sealing us within like a bank vault until morning. And do take note of the barred windows; they are there for your safety, after all." His smile was more like a sneer.

Unease settled upon the guests as they absorbed the gravity of the situation. Pritchard, meeting Loren's gaze, spoke with determination. "You know that is not possible, Mr. Loren," he stated, his words resonating with a hint of defiance.

Hawthorne furrowed his brow, considering Pritchard's words. "Are you suggesting that we are trapped inside this house, with no means of escape?" he asked, seeking clarification.

Pritchard nodded solemnly. "That's exactly what I'm saying. Mr. Loren knows it too well. Once those doors are sealed and with the windows barred, there's no getting out. They are made of solid steel, impenetrable."

A mixture of disbelief and apprehension swept through the room as the gravity of their predicament sank in. Madame Redzepova, dismissing Pritchard's concerns, scoffed defiantly. "I am not afraid of spirits, Mr. Pritchard. In fact, I converse with them every day."

Rachel Henry, chiming in with a sense of confidence, added, "I too have a connection with the other side. I am unafraid."

Jonathan Riley, his mischievous smile never fading, nodded in agreement. "Count me in as well. I'm not one to shy away from the supernatural."

Pritchard's frustration grew. "You all fail to grasp the true horror that resides within these walls. Countless murders have stained this house, some committed by our very own host." He glared at Loren, their eyes locked in a silent battle of wills.

"But I am not a ghost, Mr. Pritchard." His defiant statement hung in the air, challenging Pritchard's claims.

"Not yet," Pritchard responded, his voice filled with an eerie certainty.

Hawthorne turned his attention to Pritchard, intrigued by his knowledge of the house. "You seem to have an intimate understanding of this place. How did you come to know so much about it?"

Pritchard's gaze shifted from Hawthorne to the others in the room. "Before Mr. Loren acquired this property, I was its owner. I have experienced firsthand the horrors that dwell within these walls. This house has nearly claimed my life on two separate occasions." His hands trembled as he poured himself another glass of wine, attempting to steady his nerves with the familiar taste.

Jeannie Manning, curious to learn more, spoke up. "Please, Mr. Pritchard, enlighten us. Share your knowledge about this house and its dark history."

Loren, sensing the growing tension, decided to change the atmosphere. "Perhaps we should adjourn to the parlor, where we can discuss these matters in more comfort. Those who wish to indulge in a cocktail may do so as well." Loren looks at Stacey with a slight smile.

With a collective nod, the group rose from the dining table, their curiosity piqued by Pritchard's ominous revelations. They followed Loren towards the parlor, their minds filled with a mixture of apprehension and a desire to uncover the secrets that lay hidden within the House on Haunted Hill.

CHAPTER 8

PRITCHARD, STILL CLUTCHING his bag, spoke up, "This house was meticulously transported, stone by stone, all the way from Spain. It was originally built for Tomas de Torquemada."

Hawthorne, already skeptical of the haunted house story, replied sarcastically, "And pray tell, who is Tomas de Torquemada?"

"He was bestowed the title of First Inquisitor," Pritchard responded.

Sarah, intrigued, asked, "You mean from the era of the Spanish Inquisition?"

"Yes," Pritchard confirmed. "He had a hand in almost every major event that occurred in Spain during his lifetime. Had it not been for Torquemada, Columbus may never have sailed to the Americas, the Spanish Inquisition may never have happened, and, perhaps most importantly, 2000 Spanish citizens would never have lost their lives.

Although the exact number of Torquemada's victims remains unknown, it is widely acknowledged that he carried out several inquisitions right here, within the confines of this very house. The spirits of his unfortunate victims are said to still roam among us."

Hawthorne attempted to stifle a laugh, but his amusement was evident to everyone present.

As they made their way toward the parlor, the group passed by the house's main entrance. Suddenly, the door slammed shut, sending a surge of tension through the air, which quickly faded away. Startled, the group turned around, only to discover that the two servants had mysteriously vanished. Loren, visibly surprised by their sudden disappearance, stood up from his seat, gripping his walker, and started moving towards the door. However, Hawthorne beat him to it, reaching the door first.

"It's locked," Hawthorne states, attempting to turn the doorknob.

"They were supposed to inform me before they left," Loren remarks, a hint of disappointment in his voice.

"I want to leave, right now!" cries a hysterical Sarah Owens. She rushes towards the main entrance door, pulling on it desperately, tears streaming down her face. Hawthorne tries to pry her away, but she pulls even harder. Hawthorne then turns to Loren, his frustration evident.

"Alright, Loren. You've had your fun. Open the door so those of us who want to leave can do so. Look at the effect your haunted house is having on her,"

Hawthorne pleads, redirecting his attention back to Sarah.

Loren, still taken aback by the fact that the door is already locked, gazes at Hawthorne with a mixture of disbelief and regret. "Believe me, I wish I could open it, but as I mentioned earlier, once the doors are locked, we're all trapped here until morning," he explains.

In the midst of their conversation, the chandelier begins to sway ominously, its lights going out one by one, before crashing to the floor in a cacophony of shattered glass, narrowly missing Madame Redzepova. Jonathan Riley, unable to resist his sarcasm, remarks, "Well, Madame Redzepova, I bet you didn't see that coming." She responds with a stern glare, while Sarah rises from her seat, wiping away her tears. A tense calm settles over the room, a palpable unease filling the air.

Loren, collecting himself, addresses the group, "Maybe it's best if we make our way back to the parlor, where Mr. Pritchard can continue his captivating tale."

"Sounds like a plan. I could use a couple more drinks," Ms. Manning chimes in. They begin walking towards the parlor, but Rachel suddenly halts, pressing one hand against the wall. Curiosity aroused, she places her other hand on the wall as well. The rest of the group stops in their tracks, their gazes fixed on Rachel. Loren turns to Stacey, seeking an explanation for this peculiar behavior.

Rachel's declaration reverberates, her concentration growing more profound. Madame Redzepova responds with a dismissive scoff. "I perceive no presence in this place," she retorts, her gaze fixed on Rachel.

Suddenly, her expression morphs into one of sheer terror, and she desperately tries to retract her hands from the wall. "Help me! It's trying to drag me into the wall," she pleads, her gaze fixated on a ghostly figure manifesting within the wall. The figure appears as a man clad in tattered, dark robes, wearing a tarnished and corroded crucifix on his chest. His hands emerge from the cloak, each finger grotesquely elongated, resembling skeletal talons. To everyone's astonishment, only Rachel can see this apparition.

Hawthorne and Riley swiftly seize Rachel's hands, pulling her away from the wall, finally releasing her from its grasp. Confusion and suspicion fill the air as Rachel composes herself and directs a disdainful glare towards Redzepova. "You deceitful woman! If anyone here is a fraud, it is you."

Leaning in closer to Loren, Stacey whispers, her tone quizzical, "That wall trick was quite impressive."

Loren, taken aback, responds quietly, "I had nothing to do with it. As Madame Redzepova said, it's all part of the deception."

As the group enters the parlor, Rachel maintains a safe distance from Redzepova, her wariness evident. Unbeknownst to any of them, as they depart from the hallway, behind them a ghostly figure glides across the pathway, seamlessly passing through one wall and emerging from another. His movements are eerily graceful, each step deliberate and calculated. The very space around him seems to shrink back in fear of his malevolent presence. In his wake, chilling whispers reverberate from the walls, their words carrying a sinister and haunting tone. However, none of the occupants of the house are aware of this spectral presence lurking in their midst.

As everyone settles into their seats, Jeannie Manning takes a moment to pour herself a glass of vodka, accompanied by a few ice cubes. Following suit, Pritchard indulges in a drink while still clutching his bag. The room grows quiet, all eyes fixed on Pritchard, awaiting the continuation of his captivating narrative.

"Inside the very walls of this house," Pritchard begins, his voice filled with a haunting intensity, "countless horrifying tortures and deaths have taken place." A sly smile creeps across Loren's face as he observes the rest of the group, utterly captivated by every word flowing from Pritchard's mouth.

"During the Inquisition, Torquemada was a mastermind of cruelty and sadism, constantly devising more brutal and bloodthirsty methods to inflict pain and suffering upon the accused. He practically reinvented the art of extracting confessions from his victims."

Driven by a mix of intrigue and the effects of alcohol, Jeannie Manning interrupts, blurting out her question without realizing her own belch that followed. "What kinds of tortures did he employ?" she asks, her curiosity unfiltered.

"There were indeed many tortures inflicted by Torquemada," Pritchard responds. "Some you may be familiar with, like the strappado, where the victim's hands are bound behind their back and they are suspended, causing agonizing pain and shoulder dislocation."

Sarah, overcome with distress, exclaims, "Oh, my God. I think I'm going to be sick." She swiftly rises from her seat and exits to the hallway, with Hawthorne following close behind to provide support. Meanwhile, Pritchard continues his account.

"Of course, Torquemada employed the rack, the Judas Chair, and the Catherine Wheel, among others," he elaborates, his voice still resonating with an eerie enthusiasm.

Interrupting respectfully, Loren interjects, realizing the discomfort of his guests, "I must apologize for the unsettling nature of these vivid descriptions. To ensure the comfort of everyone present, I suggest we gather our belongings and proceed to our respective rooms. As we make our way, perhaps Mr. Pritchard can enlighten us with a guided tour. We could start in the cellar."

CHAPTER 9

"Do you really want to go down there, Mr. Loren?" Pritchard inquired, raising his eyebrow.

"Why not? I don't believe in ghosts," Loren replied confidently.

"Mr. Loren, you should heed their warning," Madame Redzepova interjected. "As Mr. Pritchard has already cautioned you, it is unwise to mock them." Her words carried a sense of seriousness. "He is correct. There are numerous entities within this house, and unfortunately, some harbor evil intentions."

Loren raises an eyebrow and displays a slight smile. "Thank you, Madame Redzepova. I will consider your advice. Now, shall we all proceed down the staircase to the cellar? Given my legs and the need for a walker, I will go last."

As the group reached the cellar, they maintained a close proximity, with Sarah positioned beside Hawthorne. Loren turned to address Pritchard, his voice filled with curiosity. "Mr. Pritchard, I have a feeling that this room harbors intriguing stories. Wouldn't you agree? Would you do us the honor?"

Pritchard's response was grave. "There is no honor to be found here, Mr. Loren. Only tormented spirits seeking vengeance." He distanced himself from the group and continued, "If you observe closely, you'll notice thirteen lamps casting their glow upon this room. Next to each lamp, you'll find storage areas designated for wine bottles and supplies. One of the previous owners had a penchant for experimenting with wine blends."

Pritchard made his way towards a wall, where a large crank awaited. He started turning it, causing a massive wooden door in the center of the floor to rise, revealing a sizable pool of liquid. Jeannie, slightly unsteady from the alcohol she had consumed, nearly lost her balance, but Riley swiftly came to her aid.

"You're lucky you didn't fall in," Pritchard exclaimed with excitement.

Jeannie, finding her balance with Riley's support, looked at Pritchard quizzically. "Why? It's just water, isn't it?"

Pritchard began scouring the area and soon came across a lifeless rat caught in a trap. Carefully retrieving the rat, he approached the vat and released it into the liquid. The contents of the vat reacted violently, frothing and bubbling as the rat's body underwent a rapid transformation, reducing to a mere skeleton floating on the surface.

Loren, unfazed by the events due to witnessing the acid's effects when his wife had fallen into the vat, as well as her lover, answered on behalf of Pritchard. "It's acid, and as you can see, it's still potent."

Pritchard glared at Loren, aware of his role in luring Annabelle to her demise in that very vat. Disgusted, he turned away from the group and led them back upstairs. Stacey, however, lingered behind to speak with Loren.

"You knew about the acid?" she inquired.

"Let's just say that both Annabelle and I were aware of it," he responded, a smirk playing on his face. Once everyone had returned upstairs, Loren guided them to their belongings. "I believe it's time to find our rooms, and on the way, Mr. Pritchard has at least one more room to show you."

The group obediently trailed Pritchard, ascending the stairs to reach the second bedroom on the left. As they stepped into the room, Hawthorne immediately voiced his confusion, "Why have we come here? It appears to be an ordinary bedroom." The space boasted a double bed, twin nightstands, a closet, and an attached bathroom.

Pritchard, visibly unsettled, swallowed before responding, "My brother met his untimely demise on the roof just above this very room. That stain you see on the ceiling is a grim reminder of his blood, lingering throughout the years."

Hawthorne and Loren exchanged dubious glances, their expressions incredulous. "You can't be serious," Hawthorne retorted, addressing Pritchard's claim. "Are you trying to say the blood is still fresh after all this time?" In that very moment, a few droplets of blood descended from above, landing on Madame Redzepova's hand. She instinctively tried to wipe it away with her other hand.

"You've been marked," Pritchard lamented with a touch of sadness. Madame Redzepova dismissed his statement as mere nonsense. Meanwhile, Rachel caught a glimpse, out of the corner of her eye, of a young girl's ethereal figure, beckoning her to follow. Sensing an inexplicable pull, Rachel quietly departed from the oblivious group, while their attention remained fixated on Madame Redzepova.

CHAPTER 10

GRACEFULLY, THE YOUNG girl's apparition glided along the hallway, seamlessly passing through the door of another room. Intrigued, Rachel pushed the door open and stepped inside, only to have it abruptly close behind her. With a surge of panic, she tugged at the door, but it stubbornly refused to yield. Realizing her predicament, Rachel turned to face the spectral presence that had led her here.

"What do you want from me?" she inquired, her voice tinged with apprehension. "Are you here to cause me harm?"

The young spirit averted her gaze and pointed towards a seemingly ordinary wall—an enigma that Rachel failed to comprehend. Suddenly, the spirit's expression shifted, filled with sheer terror and panic. "He's coming! Run!" she urgently warned. "Run! You must run!"

Perplexed by the spirit's cryptic warnings, Rachel persisted in her quest for understanding. "Who is coming?" she implored once again, seeking clarity.

The spirit locked eyes with Rachel, her expression grave, and reiterated her foreboding message, urging Rachel to flee for her own safety. However, before Rachel could react, the spirit vanished into thin air, her departure accompanied by chilling screams as if pursued by an unseen force.

Just then, the bedroom door leading to the hallway swung open, revealing Loren standing in the threshold. He swiftly informed the rest of the group that he had located Rachel. The others hurriedly made their way down the hallway, their steps hastened by a mix of concern and curiosity. Loren, leaning on his walker, stood with a perplexed expression on his face as he posed the inevitable question, "What were you doing in here?"

Rachel took a deep breath, preparing to recount her encounter, as the group eagerly gathered around Loren. "There was a young girl—a spirit," she began, her voice conveying a mix of awe and uncertainty. "She beckoned me to follow her into this room."

"She actually spoke to you?" Riley interjected, his disbelief palpable.

Madame Redzepova chimed in, her tone somber yet resolute. "It's quite possible. Spirits communicate with me frequently," she affirmed, lending credence to Rachel's extraordinary experience.

Growing increasingly weary of the ceaseless rivalry among the trio of self-proclaimed psychics, Hawthorne reached a breaking point. His frustration culminated in an outburst directed at Madame Redzepova. "Enough of this," he snapped, his voice laced with irritation. He shifted his gaze to Rachel, determined to grant her a chance to speak uninterrupted. "Go ahead," he urged, his tone softer.

Rachel offered her account in response to Hawthorne's prompting. "Initially, she simply pointed down the hallway, checking if I was following," Rachel began, her voice carrying a hint of intrigue. However, her narration was met with a scoff from Madame Redzepova, who seemed dismissive of the young girl's guidance.

"So, she led you to an empty room. Remarkable. You possess quite the talent as a psychic, my dear," Redzepova remarked sarcastically.

Undeterred by the skeptic's remark, Rachel pressed on, determined to relay her experience. "But that's not all," she continued, sidestepping Redzepova's comment. "Once we were in the room, she directed my attention towards the walls. Then, her demeanor shifted into sheer terror, and she implored me to flee. She said several times that I need to run and that someone is coming." Rachel's words hung in the air, the tension mounting as the group contemplated the implications of her encounter with the ghostly presence.

Loren's curiosity compelled him to seek further clarification. "Run? Run from what exactly? Who is coming?" he inquired, his voice laced with genuine concern.

Without hesitation, Rachel responded, her tone tinged with a mix of bewilderment and apprehension. "She didn't specify. She simply vanished, as if dissipating into thin air. However, right after, I distinctly heard a male groan and heavy footsteps approaching down the hallway. That's when the door swung open, revealing Mr. Loren standing there."

Hawthorne interrupted; his skepticism evident in his voice. "Perhaps what you heard were the sounds of Mr. Loren and the rest of us making our way down the hallway in search of you," he proposed, attempting to rationalize the unsettling sequence of events.

"But that doesn't address the appearance of the ghost she said she saw," replied Riley. Everyone looked at each other as silence filled the room.

"I believe it's best if we all make our way back to the parlor," Loren suggested, his tone laced with a hint of unease. "I have a cocktail awaiting us there. Furthermore, I propose that we stick together until we retire to our respective rooms and navigate the house in pairs. Wouldn't you agree, Mr. Pritchard?"

Pritchard maintained his silence, his expression unreadable, while he reached into his duffel bag. The group observed with startled amazement as he extracted a sizable knife, prompting a horrified gasp from Sarah. "I wonder why the ghosts didn't kill her," he mused, posing the question without expecting an answer or addressing it to anyone in particular.

"Oh, my God," Sarah exclaimed, her voice filled with alarm, echoing the shared fear that reverberated through the room. The tension in the air thickened as the group grappled with the realization of Pritchard's unexpected possession.

"I warned you, Mr. Loren, that the spirits within this house are restless," Pritchard asserted, his voice laced with a mixture of conviction and somberness. He shifted his attention to address the entire group, capturing their undivided attention. "To the best of my knowledge, this house has claimed the lives of at least seven individuals within the past five years alone. My own brother was among them. The ghosts within these walls used this very knife to dismember his body, leaving his head forever lost. The other victims suffered a similar fate. By some miracle, they found me before it was too late, but I was left barely clinging to life."

His chilling words hung in the air, casting a shroud of grim realization over the group. Slowly, they followed Loren as he led the way out of the room, proceeding down the dimly lit hallway. Hawthorne and Sarah remained behind, their expressions filled with a sense of urgency.

"After we retire to our rooms tonight," Hawthorne whispered to Sarah, his voice barely audible. "Wait for an hour, and then meet me back in this very room."

Confusion etched on her face, Sarah questioned his proposition. "Why?" she inquired, seeking clarity.

Hawthorne's eyes gleamed with a glimmer of determination. "I have a hunch, a feeling that there may be a way for us to find an escape from this place," he responded cryptically, leaving Sarah intrigued yet uncertain of what lay ahead.

CHAPTER 11

As THE GROUP reconvened in the parlor, Pritchard and Jeannie Manning eagerly accepted Loren's offer for cocktails. With a drink in hand, Loren took a moment to address the assembled guests. His voice resonated with a blend of hospitality and intrigue.

"Ladies and gentlemen, amidst the whirlwind of events thus far, we have neglected to formally introduce ourselves and share your motivations for seeking my financial support." He grins. "While some of you may already be acquainted with me and my secretary, Stacey, it is only fair that we begin with you, Mr. Hawthorne," Loren declared, gesturing towards Hawthorne to begin the introductions.

"Well, my name is John," Hawthorne began, his voice carrying the weight of his past profession. "I used to work as a homicide detective before retirement. The truth is, besides the monetary aspect, I was intrigued by the offer because of my inherent curiosity. It felt akin to participating in an escape room or a murder mystery dinner show, a chance to put my investigative skills to the test and see if I could unravel whatever you have planned for us."

Loren nodded approvingly, a glimmer of satisfaction in his eyes. "Indeed, there's nothing quite like a haunted house to challenge one's deductive abilities. So, who would like to introduce themselves next?" he inquired, inviting the others to share their motivations.

Taking the opportunity, Sarah Owens spoke up. "My name is Sarah Owens," she began, her voice carrying a mix of determination and relief. "I work as an RN at Valley General, specifically assigned to the surgical ward. I accumulated a substantial amount of student loan debt after nursing school, and this generous sum of money would go a long way in reducing that burden."

Loren listened attentively, absorbing each detail, as the introductions continued in the dimly lit parlor. "And who is next?"

"My name is Jonathan Riley. I possess psychic abilities having the unique capacity to sense and absorb the emotions of others. In the realm of parapsychology, I am commonly referred to as an empath."

As Jonathan shared their intriguing profession, Madame Redzepova visibly expressed her disdain, shaking her head in clear disapproval. The room filled with a subtle tension, highlighting the contrasting beliefs within the group.

"I am Madame Redzepova," she asserted firmly, her voice carrying a hint of defiance. "Hailing from

Macedonia, I was born with the innate ability to communicate with those who have departed this world. I have dedicated my life to this purpose, not wasting my time assessing mere emotions." Her gaze lingered on Jonathan Riley, an unspoken challenge evident in her eyes.

As the tense moment passed, Jeannie Manning cleared her throat, bringing a sense of normalcy back to the room. "Hello, my name is Jeannie Manning," she introduced herself calmly. "I work as an attorney at the Floyd, Brewster Law Firm here in the city."

Curiosity sparked in Loren's eyes as he sought to learn more. "What area of law do you specialize in, Ms. Manning?" he inquired.

Jeannie offered a warm smile before responding. "I primarily practice estate planning. My focus lies in matters of probate, trusts, and related legalities," she explained, providing a glimpse into her professional expertise.

With a sense of anticipation, Rachel Henry introduced herself as the last member to share her background. "Well, I suppose that leaves me. My name is Rachel Henry, and like Mr. Riley and Madame Redzepova, I, too, possess psychic abilities. I apologize if I struggle to pronounce your name correctly," she added, addressing Madame Redzepova respectfully. "But I must say, my abilities align closely with hers."

Driven by an overwhelming sense of pride, Madame Redzepova retorted with righteous indignation. "No soul shall ever dare to rival my extraordinary powers," she declared, her fury tangible. A tense silence enveloped the group as each member grappled with the weight of the escalating tension. Loren relished the realization that the three psychics he sought to expose were already embroiled in a heated internal conflict.

Breaking the silence, Loren interjected with a challenging tone. "That sounds like a challenge to me," he proclaimed, his eyes gleaming with intrigue. "What do the three of you psychics say to a séance, right here, right now? With the combined powers that each of you claim to possess, we should easily be able to make contact with at least one ghost among us."

The proposition lingered in the air, the room alive with a mix of skepticism, curiosity, and an undercurrent of excitement. The fate of the group seemed to hang in the balance, as they contemplated the possibility of delving deeper into the paranormal realm that surrounded the House on Haunted Hill.

Pritchard, firmly planted in his chosen spot by the fireplace, expressed his disinterest in participating. "You can count me out. I'll stay right here," he stated, clutching his knife and drink while settled in an overstuffed chair.

Turning his attention to the remaining psychics, Loren inquired about their willingness to proceed. "Well, Ms. Henry, Mr. Riley, Madame Redzepova, what do you say?" he asked, seeking their agreement.

Riley was the first to respond, his answer straightforward. "That's fine with me," he confirmed.

Loren then turned to Rachel Henry for her decision. She hesitated momentarily before relenting. "Fine," she conceded, accepting the proposition.

Lastly, Loren directed his question towards Madame Redzepova, fully aware of her confidence in her own abilities. Her response carried an air of superiority. "This is fine. My power is all that will be needed, but these two amateurs can join in and maybe learn something," she declared, asserting her dominance in the matter.

With everyone on board, Loren pointed to a large circular table in the corner of the room. Riley and Hawthorne moved it to a more suitable position, creating a central focus for the upcoming séance. Each participant took their respective seats, noticeably avoiding sitting directly next to Madame Redzepova, who seemed to take charge of the proceedings. Loren proceeded to light several candles and placed them on the table, their flickering flames casting an eerie glow.

Concerned about the lighting, Loren inquired, "Do we need to turn out the other lamps?"

"No," Madame Redzepova assured him. "They are not very bright and will not interfere. We will focus on the candles you have placed here," she declared, assuming the role of leadership for the séance. Riley and Rachel just rolled their eyes at her comment.

With everyone except Pritchard settled around the table, Madame Redzepova surveyed the group, her gaze lingering on each individual. "Now, place your baby finger next to the person to your right and left, touching their fingers," she instructed, emphasizing the physical connection between participants. Her sharp eyes scanned the table, ensuring that everyone had complied with her directive. Satisfied, she continued, "Now, we begin."

Closing her eyes, Madame Redzepova swayed gently from side to side in her seat, fully embracing the spiritual realm. Loren and Stacey exchanged a knowing glance, understanding the significance of this moment captured by the hidden recording in the cellar. As time passed, a subtle but palpable energy filled the room, causing the lamps to flicker and extinguish, enveloping the space in darkness. Only the dying embers in the fireplace and the flickering candlelight remained as sources of illumination.

Observing the gradual descent into darkness, Pritchard grew increasingly restless, his grip on the knife tightening as he braced himself for any potential threat. The dimly lit room heightened his senses, preparing him for what might come next.

"Do not break the circle," Redzepova instructed, her swaying motion unceasing. However, her sudden stillness startled everyone. The voice of a terrified young girl resonated from Redzepova's mouth, piercing the air with urgency. "You must all leave. You must all leave now. He is coming for you. Run! Run!"

Moans echoed from the walls, intertwining with piercing screams that reverberated through the room. The sporadic sound of dragging chains added to the cacophony of terror. Riley took charge, demanding answers from the unseen entity. The table began to shake and rise, prompting Sarah to scream in fear. The circle was broken, but Madame Redzepova remained entranced, continuing to channel the voice of the young spirit. "He is approaching. Flee. Flee swiftly."

The fire in the fireplace surged, causing Pritchard to spill his drink in alarm. He brandished his knife in a defensive gesture, despite the absence of a visible threat. Then, as abruptly as it had started, the energy in the room subsided. Madame Redzepova awakened, visibly shaken, while the gas lamps around the perimeter of the room flickered back to life.

"Well, that was entertaining. And what, pray tell, did you see, Madame Redzepova?" Loren asked sarcastically, his amusement evident. Still recovering from her trance, Redzepova remained silent.

"It was the same girl who led me to that empty room. She had the same voice, and she was terrified," Rachel recounted in response to Loren's question.

"Terrified is an understatement. She was petrified," Riley added, his tone conveying the seriousness of the situation.

"And what was she afraid of? Other ghosts?" Loren inquired, struggling to contain his laughter.

"Please, Mr. Loren, I need to get out of here," Sarah pleaded, seeking solace in Hawthorne's presence. Loren simply smiled before offering a suggestion to the group.

"Perhaps it's time for us to retire for the evening. I've already placed name cards on your bedroom doors, so if you'll follow me. Oh, and here's a candle for each of you in case the gas lamps go out." He distributed long black candles to each person and led them back upstairs.

"The house has over twenty-five rooms, and it's easy to get lost. Each room has its own bathroom, which is convenient. I advise that you only move through the house in pairs, if necessary. This is your room, Ms. Henry. Please make sure you lock your door."

Rachel bid everyone goodnight and retreated to her room, securing it with a lock. The rest of the group, excluding Pritchard, followed Loren's lead, continuing their journey through the mysterious house.

CHAPTER 12

STACEY, I HAVE you here and Ms. Manning you are next door. Sleep tight. Now, if the rest of you would kindly follow me," Loren directed, assuming the role of a helpful hotel assistant guiding new arrivals.

Hawthorne, finally realizing Pritchard's absence, inquired, "Where is Pritchard?"

"Oh, that peculiar little man has chosen to remain in the parlor. I suppose he prefers to stay close to the drinks," Loren replied casually. "Mr. Hawthorne, your room is right here, and Sarah, yours is next door. I assume, as a retired police detective, you are armed?" Hawthorne remained silent but exchanged a glance with Sarah.

"I hope we can rely on you if things get uneasy during the night. Mr. Riley, this is your room, and mine is just around the corner. Good night," Loren said, disappearing around the corner of the main hallway. The only one left outside the safety of locked doors was Pritchard.

A short while later, there's a soft knock on Stacey's bedroom door, and she quickly opens it. "Hurry, come in before anyone sees you," she whispers to Jeannie Manning. As soon as the door is secured, Stacey turns and pulls Manning into an embrace, their lips meeting in passionate kisses.

"Do you think he suspects anything?" Manning asks between breaths.

"Frederick? No. He's so consumed with exposing those three psychics that I'm surprised he hasn't had a heart attack already," Stacey replies. "I must say, the special effects he had his construction crew install really gives this old house the perfect atmosphere. Every room is being monitored except for mine and his."

"You know, a natural heart attack in front of all these people would be ideal for us," Jeannie suggests.

"Yes, it would, but I think we should stick to our plan. I'm certain that at some point tonight, he'll make his way down to the cellar to check what his cameras have recorded so far. When we hear him approaching the stairs, one good push should send him tumbling. Everyone here has witnessed how reliant he is on his walker. Poor man, he slipped on the stairs and broke his neck. Are you absolutely certain all the estate documents are in order?" Stacey asks, seeking reassurance.

"Everything is set to be carried out as planned. The fact that he had you sign all those documents over the years makes things much easier. After his passing, his entire estate will rightfully belong to us, Stacey," Jeannie assures her.

"Not just mine, my love, but ours," Stacey responds, their embrace continuing as they revel in their shared anticipation.

Sarah and Hawthorne cautiously enter the bedroom where Rachel claimed to have seen the young female ghost. "What exactly are we looking for?" Sarah asks, her voice filled with curiosity and apprehension.

Hawthorne pauses for a moment, collecting his thoughts. "Do you recall when Rachel mentioned that the ghost, or whatever it was, pointed to the walls?" he asks.

Sarah ponders for a moment before responding, "I was so terrified at that moment that I can't quite recall what she said."

Hawthorne nods understandingly. "Old houses like this, especially if Pritchard's claims about its origins during the Spanish Inquisition are true, often had secret passages and concealed rooms," he explains. "If Rachel's account is accurate and the apparition indeed gestured towards the walls..."

Sarah's eyes widen as realization dawns upon her. "Then it's possible that there's a hidden room or an escape route within these walls," she finishes his sentence, a glimmer of hope shining through her fear.

Hawthorne smiles, appreciating Sarah's deduction. Together, they begin to explore the room, carefully examining the walls in search of any hidden entrances or clues that may lead them to a way out of the mysterious house.

"Start tapping on the walls and see if you hear an echo," Hawthorne told Sarah. Hawthorne goes to one wall and Sarah taps on another. Nothing on the first two walls. On the third wall Sarah hears an empty echo.

"John, I think I found something. Listen." She taps on the wall and after listening, he does the same. He looks at Sarah with a smile.

"There's something behind this wall. Feel around the edges. Maybe there is some type of release mechanism."

Sarah and Hawthorne split up to search the room, each taking a different side. As Sarah presses on a baseboard, a hidden door swings inward, revealing a passage beyond. Hawthorne takes out his lighter and lights to candles giving one to Sarah. The candles casting a dim glow into the newly discovered space. Together, they cautiously step inside, finding themselves in a large, empty room covered in a thick layer of dust and cobwebs.

John turns to Sarah, a hint of determination in his eyes. "You stay here. I'm going to check out the room next door," he instructs, sensing Sarah's unease.

Sarah's apprehension is palpable as she looks at Hawthorne. "Hurry, I don't want to be alone in this dark room. It's unsettling," she confesses, her voice trembling slightly.

Understanding her concern, Hawthorne reaches into his pocket and retrieves his cigarette lighter and gives it to Sarah as an additional source of illumination.

Taking the candle in hand, Hawthorne leaves the room, the soft glow guiding his steps. As he ventures into the adjacent chamber, the sound of his footsteps reverberates through the cold and desolate space, creating an eerie atmosphere.

"Sarah, can you hear me? Hawthorne asks from the adjacent room.

"Yes, I hear you."

"Good. Let me know when you hear an echo on your side."

He begins tapping, and she listens with rapt attention. Beyond the confines of the room, the feeble gas lamps, which offered a meager sense of solace, abruptly flicker and extinguish, shrouding both the room and the concealed chamber in impenetrable darkness. Sarah's grasp on the candle tightens, its flickering glow now her sole beacon of light. Faced with a harrowing predicament, she fumbles in her pocket, desperately searching for Hawthorn's lighter but to no avail.

In the eerie half-light, she sees it—a grotesque, decaying figure emerges from the shadows. The woman is covered in blood, her long gray hair matted and disheveled. Her bony hands rise, revealing elongated, claw-like fingernails. Her joints are contorted. Sarah's scream pierces the air as terror takes hold of her, compelling her to flee the hidden room and race back into the hallway. She runs into Hawthorne.

"Sarah, what's wrong?"

"John, it was horrible (sobbing). She stood there and stared at me with this hideous grin. Her eyes were bloodshot and her fingernails looked like daggers. Her arms were all twisted. She smelled like death."

After Sarah collects herself, they both reenter the hidden room, hoping to find some evidence or clue. However, their search yields nothing. Hawthorne glances at Sarah, his expression filled with doubt, which only intensifies her frustration.

"She was there, John. I saw her, I swear," Sarah insists, desperation tinged in her voice. But Hawthorne's skeptical gaze remains, causing Sarah to feel disheartened and misunderstood. Frustration takes hold of her, and she abruptly turns away, storming out of the room.

"Sarah, wait for me," Hawthorne calls out as he follows her.

Rachel lies motionless on her bed, still dressed in her street clothes without her shoes, engrossed in a book. She still has thoughts of the confrontation with Madame Redzepova and the young female ghosts that appeared to her. The gentle glow of the wall lamp illuminates the room, casting a sense of security. But then, in an instant, darkness descends as the lamp abruptly shuts off, plunging Rachel into a chilling void. She finds her candle and lights it.

A stifled gasp escapes her trembling lips as a faint sound emerges from beneath her bed—an ominous, sinister presence lurking in the shadows. Fear paralyzes her, rendering her unable to move a muscle. The thing beneath her bed starts to ascend, its sinister intentions growing stronger.

And there, at the foot of her bed, materializes the apparition of Torquemada, the infamous ghost from the depths of history. Draped in spectral garments, he wears a stiff, ruffled collar encircling his neck like a noose. His countenance is a ghastly sight to behold—pallid, corpse-like, marked by the weight of age and the sins he committed. A deep scowl etches cruel lines upon his lips, twisted with sadistic delight. His eyes, sunken and devoid of mercy, bore into Rachel's soul, stripping her of all hope.

Rachel's terror intensifies, a vice grip of terror constricting her every fiber. Desperate to flee or scream for help, she finds herself bound by an invisible force, trapped in her own nightmare. The ghostly presence of Torquemada looms over her, his malevolence permeating the air, suffocating her with a paralyzing dread.

Within an instant, the room transforms into a nightmarish torture chamber, its walls adorned with sinister instruments of torment. Rachel, trapped in a state of disbelief, finds herself levitating from her bed, helpless against the malevolent forces at play. The restraints slither like snakes from the shadows, entwining tightly around her trembling limbs, constricting her movement.

The ghostly apparition, its eyes gleaming with sadistic pleasure, hovers ominously nearby, relishing in the unfolding horror. A ghastly presence seizes hold of the rack's crank, turning it with a malevolent intent. She sees two other inquisitors standing by her. Slowly, relentlessly, the mechanism begins to stretch Rachel's fragile body, her joints popping and grinding with grotesque intensity. Agonizing pain courses through her every nerve, her screams stifled by the malefic restraints that bind her.

In a horrifying spectacle, Rachel's limbs contort at unnatural angles, dislocating and distorting beyond recognition. The room echoes with the sickening sound of snapping bones and the haunting chorus of her tortured cries. Her body, pushed beyond the limits of endurance, succumbs to the overwhelming shock, as her heart pounds with a final desperate beat.

In the midst of the torment, Rachel's life ebbs away. The ghostly apparitions, fade into the shadows, leaving behind a chamber of eternal suffering and a life extinguished by the ultimate horror. Then the room returns to normal leaving no trace of the torture that had just taken place.

The commotion of Sarah running out into the hallway alerted everyone, drawing them to gather near her and Hawthorne. "What's going on? Is everyone okay?" Loren inquired, concerned.

"We're fine. Sarah believes she saw a ghost in a hidden room we discovered," Hawthorne explained.

"I know what I saw," Sarah asserted, her eyes fixed on Hawthorne.

"Hidden room you say. The group follows Loren to the bedroom and they all enter. From there they follow Hawthorne to the hidden chamber. Everyone looks around at the empty room. "Inconclusive, it seems," Loren remarked with a touch of disappointment. He glanced at Hawthorne, sharing a knowing smile. "Let's regroup in the parlor, Ms. Owens, and we can all gather our wits. Please, follow me."

Sarah, still visibly frustrated, stormed out of the room ahead of them. Loren exchanged a glance with Hawthorne before they both followed her, leaving the hidden chamber behind.

CHAPTER 13

As THEY ENTER the parlor Pritchard jumps up and displays his knife. "Relax Mr.

Pritchard. It is only us. No ghosts." Pritchard sits back down "Mr. Hawthorne, what prompted you and Ms. Owens to revisit that room?" Loren inquired, his curiosity evident in his tone. Hawthorne, slightly irked by the questioning, composed himself before answering.

"Given Pritchard's account of the house's history, claiming it was built during the Spanish Inquisition, I suspected the presence of hidden rooms and passageways throughout the building. We did, in fact, discover one hidden room and were in the process of further exploration when Sarah encountered the apparition."

Sarah, now seeking validation, interjected with a hint of triumph, "So, do you believe me now?"

Pritchard leaned forward in his chair, his voice filled with certainty. "Mr. Hawthorne speaks the truth. This house is teeming with secret passages and concealed chambers. The spirits that linger here have ample places to hide."

Loren, sporting a smirk on his face, countered, "But if they wish to make their presence known, why do they continue to hide? Why not reveal themselves?"

"You've mocked them, and now you challenge them," Pritchard retorted. "You won't be in this world for much longer, Mr. Loren."

"Where is Rachel?" Riley's voice cut through the tense exchange between Pritchard and Loren, his worry evident. Everyone looks around but she is not there.

"Come to think of it, she wasn't with us when we checked out that hidden room," Manning said.

"I'll go check on her," Loren said as he grabs his walker.

"I'll accompany you. Riley, I think you should stay here with the women," Hawthorne said as he caught up with Loren. Riley nodded in agreement.

They arrived at Rachel's room. Loren knocks on the door. There is no response. He knocks again. Hawthorne tries the doorknob, and it opens. They both enter. "Ms. Henry, are you alright?" Loren asks. The room is empty, but the bathroom door is closed. Loren looks at Hawthorn, who goes to the door and knocks on it. No answer. After knocking again, he slowly opens it. The bathroom is empty. They exchange puzzled glances.

Loren and Hawthorne reenter the parlor, their expressions reflecting a mixture of puzzlement and concern. "She's nowhere to be found in her room," Loren states, his voice laced with both confusion and worry. "I'm at a loss as to where she could possibly be."

Everyone is quiet until Stacey speaks up. "Alright, everyone, let's take a breath. I'm sure she'll show up. Perhaps she's exploring the house to make contact with the spirits, although that's not advisable" She smiles before continuing. "We're all stuck together until morning. I suggest we go back to our rooms, lock the doors, and stay there until tomorrow morning." Everyone looks at each other, contemplating what Stacey said.

Loren nods. "I believe that's what we should do. Does everyone agree? I know you don't, Pritchard." Prichard just ignores Loren.

Without saying anything, everyone follows Stacey back upstairs, with Loren being the last one. Everyone returns to their respective bedrooms, except for Loren. As he starts to enter, he quickly glances around the corner to ensure no one is watching, then shuts his door quietly With a determined look on his face, he quietly tiptoes down the dimly lit hallway.

Loren cautiously makes his way down a staircase that emits creaking sounds, leading him to the cellar. Memories from two decades ago flood his mind as he recalls the chilling events that unfolded here, where his unfaithful wife met her demise, slipping into a vat of acid alongside her lover, a psychiatrist. The atmosphere grows colder, and an eerie sense of foreboding envelops him as he reaches the bottom.

Surveying the room, dimly lit by thirteen flickering lights, his gaze finally settles on a concealed door.

Approaching the door shrouded in shadows, Loren deftly unlocks it with a subtle click. Slowly pushing it open, he enters a hidden chamber that reveals an assortment of cutting-edge equipment, filling the room with an air of secrecy and advanced technology.

Numerous TV monitors line the walls, displaying live feeds from various rooms of the house, including the bedrooms. Loren's eyes narrow as he focuses on Rachel Henry's room. He replays recording of her room. He sees her lying on the bed, still dressed in her street clothes, engrossed in a book. A sense of relief washes over him momentarily, but it is quickly replaced by unease.

Suddenly, the monitor's screen for Henry's room abruptly turns black, plunging the room into darkness. After several tense moments, the screens flicker back to life showing an empty room. Rachel Henry is nowhere to be seen. Loren's brow furrows with concern and confusion. He replays it a second and third time.

Pritchard, still nursing his drink in the parlor, tightly grips his knife as Sarah Owens and Hawthorn make their entrance. Startled, Pritchard swiftly turns his chair to face them, brandishing the knife. "Why have you ventured out of your rooms?" he demands.

"Take it easy, Pritchard. We simply wish to inquire further about this house," Hawthorne responds calmly.

"It's too late. The spirits are enraged with Mr. Loren and the rest of you. We won't survive until morning." Pritchard's words carry a sense of impending doom.

Hawthorne, feeling frustrated, pauses for a moment before speaking up. "Listen, Pritchard, I'm a retired cop, and I don't believe in ghosts. But maybe, with your assistance, we can find a way to escape this place. Please, tell us everything you know about the house."

"I've already told you," Pritchard begins. "This house was constructed for Torquemada, the First Inquisitor. Legend has it that he used this very place to carry out his interrogations in utmost secrecy."

"Why the need for secrecy?" Hawthorne inquires.

"Torquemada was a sadistic man," Pritchard reveals with a grim expression. "It's said that he would abduct young women, subject them to his desires, and then mercilessly torture them to their deaths."

Sarah gasps, her hand instinctively covering her mouth, overcome with horror at the gruesome revelation.

"Is there any information about how many victims he had or where in the house he carried out these acts?" Hawthorne asks with a mix of curiosity and unease.

"No one truly knows," Pritchard responds. "According to the legends, he frequented the cellar extensively. Some claim that he expanded the house, adding rooms dedicated to specific methods of torture. The rack, the Catherine Wheel... you name it."

"I have no desire to know or dwell on the details," Sarah interjects firmly. "All I want is to find a way out of this house."

Undeterred by Sarah's statement, Pritchard continues, seemingly unaffected. "Torquemada descended into madness, you see. People began circulating tales of his insatiable thirst for blood. In fact, in June 1494, Pope Alexander VI had to appoint four assistant inquisitors to rein him in. Some even accused him of dabbling in witchcraft, which may have contributed to his descent into madness. Who can say for certain?"

Hawthorne signals to Sarah, gesturing for her to join him in a secluded spot away from Pritchard, who appears deep in contemplation. Leaning closer to her, he whispers softly, "I believe we should return to the room where you encountered the ghost. Consider this: do you recall when Rachel mentioned that a young girl pointed to the wall before disappearing?"

Curiosity piqued, Sarah asks, "What are you thinking?"

"I'm hoping that the answers we seek may lie within those very walls," Hawthorne responds. Determination gleams in his eyes as he adds, "This time, we'll remain together." He discreetly reveals his weapon, concealed beneath his jacket.

CHAPTER 14

RILEY PEACEFULLY SLUMBERS, lost in the depths of a profound sleep, his dreams filled with grandiose visions of showcasing his talent, even if it meant relying on cunning tricks. Suddenly, a stirring sensation rips him from his slumber, alerting him to an unsettling disturbance in the room. His eyes flutter open, only to behold the bed comforter gradually ascending. Fear grips him, rendering him immobile and unable to move a muscle.

In a sudden burst of violence, the comforter is forcefully ripped away from Riley, sending waves of panic coursing through his veins. Desperate to scream, he finds his voice stifled, unable to produce any sound. Hovering above him, an ominous presence materializes—the ghostly figure of Torquemada. A wicked smile twists across Torquemada's face, emanating an eerie aura.

The room undergoes a grotesque transformation, twisting into a nightmarish torture chamber. Riley's terror-stricken eyes widen as he beholds the horrifying scene unfolding before him. Dominating the center of the room is a gruesome Catherine Wheel, while two other inquisitors, concealed by black robes, stand nearby.

Riley's body is seized by the two inquisitors, their ominous garments billowing ominously. With relentless determination, they carry him towards the dreadful Catherine Wheel, casting a foreboding shadow over the room. Riley's limbs are forcibly bound to the wheel, his futile struggles met with unyielding resistance.

Under the command of one of the inquisitors, the merciless rotation of the wheel commences. Riley's anguished face contorts with unbearable pain as the restraints tighten, slicing into his flesh. His desperate attempts to scream are suffocated, silenced by an invisible force. Torquemada gazes upon the spectacle, a sinister grin etched upon his face.

Sounds of ligaments tearing, muscles rending, and bones snapping blend with Riley's stifled cries. As his life slips away, his body succumbs to the brutality inflicted upon it. The room trembles, resonating with a final crescendo of terror, accompanied by a malevolent laugh from Torquemada. Abruptly, silence descends upon the room. The wheel halts its relentless turning, and the inquisitors retreat into the shadows.

Gradually, the room reverts to its previous state of normalcy, as if the horrifying events had never transpired within its walls. The bed lies empty, devoid of any trace of Riley's existence. His life has been extinguished, his presence obliterated, leaving behind an eerie emptiness.

With utmost caution, Hawthorne and Sarah venture into the room where the haunting vision had manifested before Sarah's eyes. Their gaze meticulously scans every corner, alert to any hidden mysteries that may lie within. Once again, Hawthorne entrusts his cigarette lighter to Sarah, instructing her, "Hold this," before igniting the flame. "We stay together. We'll be alright. There's something in this room that the young girl wanted us to uncover."

Shoulder to shoulder, they initiate a methodical process of tapping on the walls, their aim to unveil any concealed secrets that might be lurking within. Suddenly, a distinct thud resonates through the room, immediately seizing their attention. "There's something behind this wall," John declares, a note of anticipation in his voice.

Hawthorne retrieves his semi-automatic firearm, carefully removing the clip for added precaution. Using the butt of the gun, he begins forcefully striking the wall, causing the sheetrock to crack and crumble, ultimately creating an opening through which they can explore further.

"Pass me the lighter," Hawthorne requests, and Sarah promptly hands it over. Hawthorne directs the beam of light into the newly created gap in the wall. "There's a bookcase back here," he reveals, his voice brimming with excitement. Determinedly, they continue removing sheetrock from the wall, steadily revealing a path leading to the hidden bookcase. After some effort, they finally reach through and extract a sizable, ancient-looking bound book.

A surge of anticipation fills the room as Hawthorne successfully retrieves the enigmatic item. They retreat into the main bedroom, where the illumination is comparatively better, allowing for a closer examination of the book. With bated breath, they carefully inspect its weathered pages, eager to uncover the secrets that lie within.

"Can you read it?" John inquires, his curiosity piqued.

With unwavering determination, Sarah responds, her voice brimming with a mix of anticipation and astonishment. "I had four years of high school Spanish and another three in college. Let's see if I can recall any of it." As she gazes upon the opening pages of the ancient book, her eyes widen with a profound realization.

"Oh my God," Sarah exclaims, her voice filled with astonishment. "This is a record of the court of the Inquisition. It meticulously documents the names of the accused and the charges they faced—blasphemy, heresy, sodomy, sorcery." Her voice quivers with a mix of fascination and unease as she continues, her gaze locked onto the pages before her. "Look here... it unveils a chilling revelation. In just one year, an astounding number of individuals, 2,000 of them, were accused of sorcery and witchcraft, only to meet their fate by being burned alive at the stake."

Consumed by an insatiable curiosity, Sarah meticulously scans the book's pages until she arrives at its middle, her anticipation growing as she yearns to unveil further hidden secrets. "This is actually two books in one," she reveals, her voice tinged with intrigue. "The first part is the official record of the Inquisition. Interesting."

Hawthorne, eager to understand, queries, "What is it?"

Sarah's eyes widen as she makes a chilling discovery within the second part of the book. "The second part documents the activities within this very house," she explains, her tone laced with a mix of shock and disgust. "If this is the work of Torquemada, then Pritchard was right. All of these victims were young females... 11 years old, 10 years old, 13 years old." She pauses as she continues to scan the text. "My God. Not one of the victims were over 25 years old." A sense of revulsion colors her words. "This man was truly sick, pardon my French." Hawthorne smiled at Sarah's apparent distaste for profanity.

As John grapples with the unsettling revelation shared by Sarah, his mind races to comprehend the intentions behind the young girl's cryptic message. "But why did she want Rachel to discover this?" he ponders aloud, his voice tinged with confusion.

"It doesn't offer us an escape plan or any useful information."

Suddenly, the ambiance of the room takes a sinister turn. One by one, the lamps flicker and extinguish, shrouding the space in darkness. A ghostly presence begins to emerge from the very floor itself, sending shivers down their spines. Reacting swiftly, Sarah rushes towards Hawthorne, seeking refuge in his presence, while he instinctively retrieves his gun, prepared to defend against the unknown entity.

A chilling presence materializes before them—a young girl clad in tattered 12th-century garments, the fabric stained and encrusted with dried blood. Her hair was matted, and she smelled of decay. The signs of torment and suffering were unmistakable. In an ethereal display, she floats past Hawthorne and Sarah, drawing their attention towards the concealed room.

Not feeling threatened, Hawthorne rebolsters his weapon but keeps Sarah close by his side. Raising her hand, the apparition points to an adjacent wall, her gesture laden with eerie significance. Then, with a voice that sends shivers down their spines, she utters a terrifying warning, "You need to leave. He will come for you. You must escape this house."

The gravity of the girl's foreboding message hangs heavy in the room, saturating the atmosphere with an unsettling unease that can almost be touched. As she vanishes into thin air, Hawthorne and Sarah exchange perplexed glances, their thoughts entangled in an attempt to grasp the haunting encounter they have just witnessed. Sarah slowly loosens her hold on Hawthorne, while he calmly reassures himself by patting his shoulder harness, ensuring the presence of his weapon.

Regaining their composure, the pair lock eyes, silently acknowledging the gravity of the situation. Determined to uncover the truth, they resolutely turn their attention to the wall that the spirit had ominously pointed towards. With a shared sense of purpose, they cautiously begin tapping on the designated area, driven by the desperate hope of unraveling the mysteries that surround them.

Loren stands in the interior hallway, rapping gently on Stacey's door. It creaks open slowly, revealing Stacey's concerned face. "What happened now?" she inquires, her voice laced with worry.

"Let's just say things are not going as planned," Loren responds with a tinge of frustration evident in his voice.

Stacey ponders Loren's cryptic reply for a moment before posing another question. "Have you found Rachel Henry?" she asks, her curiosity piqued.

Loren's gaze turns distant as he recalls his recent activities. "No. I just came from the cellar and checked the monitors," he states, seemingly lost in thought.

Stacey raises an eyebrow, surprised that Loren ventured into the cellar alone. "You did? I didn't hear you leave your room. Did you notice anything unusual in Rachel's bedroom?" she asks, concern etched across her face.

"That's the strangest part," Loren begins, his tone tinged with perplexity. "I saw Ms. Henry lying on her bed, engrossed in a book. Then, suddenly, the monitor went black for several minutes. When it came back on, the room was empty."

Stacey's eyes widen, mirroring the growing apprehension within her. "What do you think happened to her?" she inquires, her voice filled with genuine concern.

"I have no idea," Loren admits, a hint of unease creeping into his voice. "All the other guests are accounted for. It's the weirdest thing. But don't worry, are you alright?" he asks, shifting his focus to Stacey's well-being.

"Yes, Frederick," Stacey responds, using Loren's given name. "Just promise me that you'll be careful when going up and down those stairs to the cellar. Better yet, next time you plan on going down there, come and get me."

Loren's lips curl into a warm smile at Stacey's protective nature. "Always looking out for me, aren't you?" he remarks, a touch of gratitude in his voice.

Steam envelops the bathroom as Redzepova, draped in a robe, busies herself with preparing a bath. Peering into the mirror, she finds it fogged up and promptly wipes it clear, only to discover an empty medicine cabinet behind it. Slowly shutting the cabinet door, she catches sight of a young girl's face in the reflection. A ghostly apparition stands before her.

"You must hide. He is coming," the young girl's voice warns before vanishing into thin air. Redzepova takes a deep breath, composing herself, before addressing the empty space in a resolute tone. "Nonsense, young lady. I am here to confront him, whoever he may be, and bring him the peace he needs."

With determination burning in her eyes, Redzepova prepares to face the unknown entity, steadfast in her mission to unravel the mysteries and put restless spirits to rest. She undresses and gracefully steps into the warm water of the bathtub. Placing a washcloth over her eyes, she hums a soothing melody.

Unbeknownst to her, the presence of Torquemada materializes, gradually entering the room through the closed door. His ominous figure is accompanied by two other inquisitors. They stare at Redzepova. Madame Redzepova's humming falters as she senses a shift in the temperature of the room. Suddenly, a forceful hand descends upon the crown of her head, mercilessly pushing her beneath the water's surface. Panic sets in as she fights desperately for air, her survival instincts kicking in.

She struggles with every ounce of strength, battling against the relentless pressure on her head. But exhaustion takes hold, weakening her resolve. Her resistance wanes until she succumbs to the overpowering force, her body becoming limp and seemingly lifeless.

In a chilling moment, the hand releases its grip, and Redzepova is pulled from the bath, now unconscious in the clutches of the relentless spirits. In a few seconds Redzepova awakens, her surroundings transformed into a nightmarish torture chamber. Her room, once familiar and comforting, now holds sinister secrets. She finds herself dressed in a ghastly purple gown.

Hanging below her is a menacing device known as the Judas Cradle, a wooden pyramid-shaped seat designed for unspeakable torment. Redzepova is suspended, her body positioned with the apex of the pyramid aimed precisely between her legs. Her hands and legs are bound, leaving her unable to shift her weight or escape the impending horror.

A wave of dread washes over her as she becomes acutely aware of the pointed edge of the pyramid slowly penetrating her most intimate area. Torquemada, the orchestrator of this sadistic performance, revels in his sadistic amusement, his laughter echoing through the chamber. His two assistants assist in lowering Redzepova, intensifying her excruciating descent onto the unforgiving seat.

As the torment continues, blood begins to drip onto the floor. In a matter of minutes, Madame Redzepova succumbs to her torturous fate, her life extinguished. Torquemada has a sinister grin on his face as he slowly rises through the ceiling. As the final inquisitor vanishes, the room returns to normal.

CHAPTER 15

HAWTHORNE AND SARAH'S determination remains unwavering as they persistently tap on the walls, driven by a growing urgency. Suddenly, a distinct thud resonates through the room, capturing their undivided attention. Their eyes lock, filled with a glimmer of anticipation and a shared understanding.

Reacting swiftly, Hawthorne retrieves his gun once more, his grip firm and resolute. He removes the clip form his semi-automatic and begins delivers forceful strikes to the sheetrock, causing it to crack and crumble, revealing a hidden compartment that has remained concealed for ages. As the dust settles, a glimpse of the past is unveiled before them.

Their gazes fixate on a solitary manuscript, its pages adorned with cobwebs and layers of dust, untouched by human hands for countless years. A large spider scurries across its surface, a silent guardian of forgotten knowledge. Hawthorne and Sarah exchange a knowing look, recognizing the significance of their discovery.

With utmost care, Hawthorne brushes away the spider and delicately clears the cobwebs, revealing the ancient manuscript in all its aged glory. He blows gently on the cover, sending a cloud of dust swirling through the air. Extending his hand, he presents the precious artifact to Sarah, who accepts it with reverence.

Sarah opens the weathered pages of the manuscript, each one filled with faded ink and the secrets of the past waiting to be unveiled. The room becomes hushed as they delve into the depths of history, their hearts pounding with anticipation and their minds racing with possibilities.

"This text holds a different purpose," Sarah remarks, her voice filled with intrigue. "It outlines a series of rituals and actions that have the potential to weaken and ultimately vanquish a spirit."

Hawthorne's expression shifts to one of understanding and determination. "Very well," he responds with a nod. "Let us convene in the parlor. We must share this newfound knowledge with everyone and devise a comprehensive plan."

With a shared sense of urgency, Hawthorne and Sarah leave the room, carefully carrying the ancient manuscript with them. As they make their way to the parlor, their minds race with the possibilities that lie ahead, hoping that the gathered group will find solace in the information and unite in their efforts to overcome the malevolent forces that surround them.

Jeannie discreetly knocks on the door, and Stacey opens it with caution. "Come in quickly. Did anyone see you?" Stacey asks, her voice filled with a mixture of concern and anticipation.

"No need to worry. Soon we'll have a fortune in our hands," Jeannie reassures, her eyes gleaming with excitement and secrecy. They share a brief embrace, their minds filled with the possibilities that lie ahead. "But we must hurry. It's already three in the morning. When will Frederick make a trip to the cellar?"

"He went down there around an hour ago. I haven't heard him leave his room since then," Stacey replies, contemplating their next move. "I'll have to come up with a reason for him to venture down again."

As the weight of their secret mission hangs in the air, Jeannie and Stacey exchange determined glances, knowing that their plan hinges on Frederick's unwitting involvement. Time becomes their ally and their enemy, as they plot their next move with careful consideration, aware that the success of their endeavor relies on their ability to orchestrate events without raising suspicion.

Hawthorne and Sarah reenter the parlor with the expectation of finding everyone gathered, but to their surprise, only Pritchard is there. "Where is everyone?" Hawthorne inquires.

"In their rooms, where the two of you should also be. The spirits are becoming increasingly restless," Pritchard responds, his knife held prominently, underlining the seriousness of the situation. Hawthorne exchanges a brief glance with Sarah.

"Stay here with Pritchard. I'll go gather everyone," Hawthorne instructs before stepping out, leaving Sarah with an uneasy feeling in Pritchard's presence. She positions herself near him, maintaining a watchful stance.

Hawthorne raps on Loren's door, and he opens it with an anxious expression. "Is everyone okay? Has Rachel come back?" Loren queries immediately upon greeting Hawthorne at his doorstep.

"I haven't heard anything. Sarah, ah, Ms. Owens, and I have discovered something that could aid our escape from this house. I'm attempting to gather everyone in the parlor," Hawthorne explains.

Loren firmly stabilizes his walker and closes his door, moving gradually towards Jonathan Riley's room. He knocks, but there's no response. Taking the lead, Hawthorne opens the door, unveiling an empty room. They proceed to Madame Redzepova's room and knock, but once again, there is no answer. They cautiously enter the room, only to find it also vacant.

"Mr. Loren, this situation has escalated to a dangerous point. Someone is likely to get injured. You must cancel this haunted house party," Hawthorne implores.

"Mr. Hawthorne, I truly wish I could. However, it appears that circumstances have spiraled beyond my ability to control," Loren responds with a hint of resignation.

"What do you mean?"

"I must confess, I staged a few haunted house effects to expose our supposed psychics. I wanted to prove to the world that they were nothing but frauds."

"So, the ghosts that Sarah and Rachel claimed to see were actually your contraptions?"

"No, Mr. Hawthorne. That's precisely what I've been attempting to convey. The only special effects I arranged were the crashing chandelier and the closing of the main entrance door. However, everything we're witnessing now seems to be originating from the house itself," Loren clarifies. They exchange concerned glances, realizing that the malevolent forces at play are far beyond their expectations.

"We must check on Stacey and Ms. Manning," Loren declares, initiating his journey down the hallway towards their respective rooms.

Later, Stacey, Manning, Hawthorne, and Loren enter the parlor, reuniting with Pritchard and Sarah. "Where are Madame Redzepova and Mr. Riley?" Sarah inquires.

"They're not in their rooms. We assumed they were already here with you," Hawthorne responds.

"Have they vanished too?" Sarah asks, her voice trembling with fear as she edges closer to Hawthorne for comfort.

"The spirits have taken them. They're drawing nearer," Pritchard shouts, his words slurred due to his intoxicated state.

Loren turns to Stacey and Jeannie Manning. "Ms. Owens and Mr. Hawthorne have come across a potential means of escape from this house," Loren says. Hawthorne and Sarah place two books on the table. John is the first to break the silence.

"We stumbled upon these in the hidden room upstairs. The first book is divided into two parts. The initial section contains an official account of the Spanish Inquisition led by Torquemada, while the second half details the numerous murders he committed within this very house. His victims were all young girls."

The group congregates around Sarah and Hawthorne, with Pritchard included. Sarah directs their attention to the smaller book. "This book contains a collection of rituals, but most importantly, it provides detailed instructions on how to exorcise Torquemada's spirit from the house," she explains.

Within the cellar, moans and screams reverberate through the walls. The lamps dim and extinguish, one after another. The door concealing the vat of acid rises, unveiling its contents. Unseen by those in the parlor, spirits clad as inquisitors, accompanied by the ghostly presence of Torquemada, start to roam, casting an eerie atmosphere throughout the house.

CHAPTER 16

INSIDE THE PARLOR, Sarah remains engrossed in the smaller book, flipping through its pages. "According to this passage," she explains, "there is a sacred relic concealed within the house. It is believed to possess the ability to weaken Torquemada. Look, here is a drawing." The group converges around Sarah, their attention captivated by the illustration. The drawing depicts an exquisite pendant, adorned with intricate swirls and ancient symbols intertwining in elaborate patterns.

"Ladies and gentlemen, I must voice my doubts regarding the entirety of this situation. I am inclined to believe that our three self-proclaimed psychics have orchestrated their own vanishing act. It is highly likely that they became aware of my intentions to unveil their fraudulent practices to the world. Without a doubt, they are concealed somewhere within this very house," he asserts with skepticism.

"If that's the case, Mr. Loren, there's a chance we may come across them while searching for the relic.

It would be prudent for us to remain together in groups," Hawthorne suggests.

"Ms. Manning and I can join Frederick in his search, while the three of you can form another group," Stacey says, looking at Hawthorne, Sarah, and Pritchard.

"You're all utterly insane. I refuse to venture any deeper into this house. Mr. Loren, you're mistaken. The spirits have already taken Madame Redzepova, Riley, and Henry. They will continue to eliminate us, one by one," Pritchard declares anxiously.

"Very well, Pritchard. If you insist on staying behind with your knife and alcohol, then so be it," Hawthorne concedes as they divide into two groups.

Just before parting ways, Hawthorne offers another suggestion. "We won't be able to communicate with you or determine if you've succeeded in locating the relic. Let's agree to reconvene here in one hour, and we can evaluate which areas of the house still need to be searched."

The group splits into two, resolved to face the supernatural challenges ahead. With a mix of determination, fear, and a glimmer of hope, they disperse into the eerie depths of the haunted house.

Sarah and Hawthorne proceed cautiously through a sinister corridor, their senses on high alert. Suddenly, a noise catches their attention, causing them to swiftly pivot around. From the wall, a figure materializes in an abrupt manner. It is the tormented apparition of

Madame Redzpova, her visage twisted and distorted. She extends a spectral hand toward them, her eyes conveying a mix of desperation and cautionary intent.

From the spirit of Madame Redzepova emerges an eerie voice, resonating with a haunting tone. "Stop! You must not advance any further. He awaits your arrival. The relic you seek harbors the key to our everlasting torment. Retreat, or you shall succumb to the same cruel fate as ours."

Sarah, although still gripped by fear, musters newfound courage and addresses the spirit.

"We understand the torment that consumes this dwelling. Our purpose is to shatter the cycle, to free you and the tormented spirits from their eternal anguish," she declares with conviction.

Hawthorne joins in, reinforcing their intent. "With the relic in our possession, we strive to restore harmony and provide solace to those who have endured immeasurable pain."

The ethereal form of Madame Redzpova's apparition flickers, caught between the impulse to shield them and the realization of their genuine intentions. Gradually, she withdraws her spectral hand and dissipates like mist, vanishing into the atmosphere.

Loren arrives at the top of the stairs that descend into the cellar, leaving his walker behind. Jeannie Manning follows closely behind, with Stacey trailing behind her. Manning glances over her shoulder at Stacey, who nods in agreement. Manning begins to push Loren forward, but in a sudden twist of events, Loren swiftly turns around, causing Manning to lose balance and tumble down the stairs, resulting in a fatal injury to her neck. Stacey lets out a piercing scream and rushes past Loren to the lifeless body of Manning. She places Manning's head in her lap and then turns her gaze towards Loren, a mix of shock, horror, and accusation etched upon her face.

"You killed her, you murderer," accuses Stacey, a hateful smile creeping across her face as she descends the staircase with a deliberate pace. Stacey, filled with shock and disbelief, musters a shaky response trying to gather her wits.

"Come now my dear Stacey. This was a staged attempt on my life. Even Annabelle would be proud of your attempt."

Confusion etches Stacey's face as she tries to comprehend his accusations. "Loren, I don't understand. What are you talking about?"

"At first, I dismissed my suspicions when you selected Ms. Manning as one of my guests. I wondered why, out of all those who responded to my invitations, that you specifically selected her?"

"You have it all wrong Frederick. It was just by chance that I found her returned interest card indicating that she wanted to come to your haunted house party. We were just good friends and I thought that with her gambling debt, this would be a good way of helping a friend out."

Loren's smile widens, a chilling glint in his eyes. "I find it hard to believe it was mere chance. You've been acting suspiciously, and I've been connecting the dots."

Loren's voice takes on a menacing tone. "Your bedroom in this house isn't under surveillance, but the hallways are." Stacey's mind races as she recalls the two private meetings she had with Manning in her room, away from prying eyes.

"You had secretive encounters with Manning in your room, behind closed doors. I wondered what that was all about," Loren asserts, raising an eyebrow.

Stacey stammers nervously, attempting to justify their meetings. "Loren, you're being paranoid. Jeannie, I mean Ms. Manning, and I are friends. We were just catching up. I wanted her to have a chance to win your $100,000 prize. That's all."

Loren's smile remains, his doubt evident. "Friends don't conspire behind closed doors, Stacey."

Stacey's unease grows as Loren delves deeper into his accusations. "I've also been contemplating how you've been signing my legal documents all these years, forging my signature. That is when it all fit together."

Stacey's nerves escalate, her words faltering. "Loren, I... I can explain. It was for your own benefit. I was taking care of things while you were absent."

Loren's voice drips with scorn. "Taking care of things, like forging my signature on new trust documents to ensure you inherit my wealth upon my demise?"

Stacey stutters, attempting to defend herself. "Loren, you're mistaken. I would never..."

"Don't lie to me, Stacey. I've connected the dots. The House on Haunted Hill invitation, your clandestine meeting with Manning... It's was all a part of a plot to murder me," Loren accuses, his smile unyielding. Stacey continues to retreat, fear enveloping her. Unbeknownst to her, the door concealing the vat of acid behind her starts to rise, revealing the treacherous chasm beneath it.

In her desperation to distance herself from Loren's approaching figure, Stacey's foot slips on a slick patch of the floor. Her arms flail momentarily, but she fails to regain her balance. With a startled cry, she hurtles backward, her body careening towards the gaping doorway of the vat of acid. The splash of her body echoed in the large cellar room. The acid bubbles ominously as Stacey's body disappears into the abyss, vanishing with a dreadful splash. Moments later, her bones resurface, a grim testament to her tragic fate.

The room descended into an unsettling stillness, the weight of the moment heavy in the air, punctuated only by the faint hiss of the acid below. Loren's eyes remained fixed on the spot where Stacey had vanished, a mixture of cold calculation and satisfaction dancing in his gaze. With a chilling determination, he approached the lifeless body of Ms. Manning and began to drag her towards the open vat.

HOUSE ON HAUNTED HILL: RESURRECTION

The sound of his footsteps echoed ominously against the walls as he lowered her limp form into the depths of the acid, the ghastly liquid greedily consuming her remains. A perverse satisfaction emanated from Loren, his actions revealing a depth of darkness within him that few could fathom.

As he stepped back, the realization of what he had done settled upon him. The room seemed to shrink in on itself, suffocating him with the weight of his own malevolence. The once familiar cellar now bore witness to a sinister secret, hidden beneath a façade of ghostly hauntings.

Loren's gaze darted anxiously across the room, as the dancing shadows played tricks on his weary mind. He was acutely aware that his own choices had sealed his fate, forever intertwining his existence with the ominous legacy of the house. The spirits that once yearned for liberation now became his eternal companions within its walls. Faint groans and whispers seemed to echo in his ears, but he forcefully dismissed them from his consciousness, unwilling to succumb to their haunting presence.

A shiver ran down his spine as he contemplated the horrifying truth—he had become the very monster he had sought to vanquish. And as the acid continued to bubble and churn, Loren realized that the House on Haunted Hill held more than just ghosts; it held the echoes of his own sins, forever etched into its cursed walls. As he strolled away, he glances back and utters, "Give my regards to Annabelle, ladies."

Sarah and Hawthorne cautiously navigate the dimly lit corridor, their every step resonating in the eerie silence. Their trepidation grows as they approach a closed door. "Let's give this one a try," Hawthorne suggests.

Just as Hawthorne extends his hand toward the doorknob, a deep groan ripples through the hallway, causing both to freeze in their tracks. Their eyes widen in alarm as the carpet before them starts to rise and writhe, resembling a sentient being, slithering closer with a disquieting intent. Hawthorne pulls out his gun.

Unfazed by the unnerving sight before them, they push open the door and step inside, their hearts pounding in their chests. Hawthorne's grip tightens around his gun, prepared for whatever awaits them on the other side. With a resolute thud, Hawthorne forcefully slams the door shut behind them, cutting off their escape route but keeping whatever is on the outside at bay.

Suddenly, the door shudders violently, rattling on its hinges, but then an eerie silence descends, freezing the door in place and taunting them with its deceptive stillness. Hawthorne remains steadfast, leaning his weight against the door to fortify it against whatever lurks beyond. "What... what is happening?" Sarah's voice trembles with terror. Yet, just as abruptly as the disturbance subsided, it surges back with even greater force, jolting them both. Then, as swiftly as it began, it abruptly ceases once more, leaving them in bewildered silence.

"I'm not entirely certain, Sarah," Hawthorne admits, his voice laced with uncertainty. "Perhaps it's Torquemada. However, it appears that whatever entity was responsible... it has vanished, at least for the time being." They exchange a knowing look, acknowledging that their encounter with the enigmatic force within the hallway was far from happenstance.

After gathering their wits, Hawthorne suggested to check on another room. However, their search proves fruitless, and with the hour nearly elapsed, they concede to returning to the parlor. As Sarah and Hawthorne make their way back to the parlor, they find Pritchard already present.

Just then, Loren enters the room. "Mr. Loren, are Stacey and Ms. Manning not with you?" Sarah inquires, her concern evident.

"I thought they had returned here already. We split up to cover more ground," Loren replies with a hint of worry.

Pritchard's gaze fixates on them, his hand gently caressing the large knife in his possession. "One by one," he murmurs, a chilling undertone in his voice. "I warned you. One by one."

"Listen carefully. We must locate that relic," Hawthorne declared urgently, his voice filled with determination. "Sarah and I witnessed something otherworldly, and time is running out. We must persist in our search."

Pritchard rises unsteadily from his chair, inadvertently spilling his drink in the process. "Let me see that drawing again," he requests, studying it intently. "You know, I've been inside this haunted house on two previous occasions, and I swear I've encountered this image before."

"Where, Pritchard? Think, man," Hawthorne implores with frustration, gripping Pritchard's shoulders firmly. "Focus. If there's a relic that can aid us, we need to find it. Tell us where you saw it."

"I'm trying, I'm trying," Pritchard replies, gradually regaining his composure and clarity of thought. "It's in the library. Yes, that's where I glimpsed it. I distinctly remember a hidden compartment behind a portrait of Torquemada as I hid from the ghosts."

Sarah approaches Pritchard with a calm demeanor. "Mr. Pritchard, can you recall the location of the library?" she asks gently. Pritchard remains unresponsive, seemingly lost in his own contemplations.

Loren steps forward, his voice carrying authority. "I remember the way to the library, Mr.

Pritchard, this time I believe you need to accompany us," he states firmly. Pritchard agrees and the group exits the parlor, making their way through the winding corridors of the haunted house.

With newfound focus and a sobering resolve, Pritchard takes charge, assuming the leadership role from Loren. He guides them forward with a sense of purpose, his knife held steadily in front of him, ready to face whatever challenges lie ahead.

CHAPTER 17

Pritchard guided the group through the dimly lit upper hallway, their destination set on the library. Suddenly, a dense mist begins to seep out from a wall, filling the air with an ominous presence. The temperature in the area dropped dramatically.

A grotesque and menacing apparition of an inquisitor materializes before them, it's very essence exuding malice. "You shall not obtain what you seek. This house shall be your eternal prison," it hisses with a spectral voice, a chilling declaration of their impending fate.

Sarah's eyes widen in sheer terror as the ghostly figure solidifies, its ethereal hands stretching out toward her, grasping at her ankle. She lets out a piercing scream, her fear palpable in the air. Pritchard brandishes his knife, but his drunken efforts of striking the apparition proved futile against the spectral entity.

Reacting swiftly, Loren and Hawthorne rush to Sarah's aid, swiftly freeing her from the clutches of the spectral form. The apparition hisses in anger as it retreats back into the wall, its threat temporarily repelled.

"Are you alright?" Hawthorne asks, concern etched on his face as he examines Sarah's ankle, finding no visible injury.

"I'm fine," Sarah assures him, her voice trembling slightly with residual fear.

"Here we are," Pritchard announces, leading them into the library. The room sprawls before them, adorned with towering bookshelves that exude an air of haunting mystery. Pritchard strides purposefully toward the large portrait of Torquemada, hanging prominently on the wall. "Here... behind this portrait... there's a hidden compartment," he reveals, his voice filled with anticipation.

Hawthorne and Sarah swiftly join Pritchard's side, their eyes fixed on the portrait. "So, that is what Torquemada looked like?" Loren asked no one in particular. With synchronized efforts, they pull on the edges of the heavy frame, unveiling a secret compartment concealed behind it. Within the compartment, they find the long-sought relic. Sarah's hand reaches out, her fingers closing around the artifact, her grip firm with determination.

"This is it... the relic. The key to banishing the evil spirits from this house," Sarah says in amazement.

"Let's get back to the parlor," Hawthorne commands.

From the very floor, a ghostly figure emerges, its ethereal form taking shape before their eyes. With a furious lunge, it hurtles toward Pritchard, extending an arm adorned with a menacing, claw-like hand. Pritchard's reflexes kick in, and he reacts swiftly, swinging his knife in a deft motion, slashing through the spectral arm.

The severed limb tumbles to the ground, twitching momentarily before being engulfed and absorbed back into the swirling mist. The apparition releases a bone-chilling scream that reverberates through the room before gradually dissolving into nothingness, leaving only an eerie silence in its wake.

With a proud and determined stance, Pritchard declares, "That's for my brother, you asshole!"

As they regroup in the parlor, Pritchard makes his way back to the bar, his mind pondering their next course of action. Loren breaks the silence, voicing the question that hangs in the air. "Now that we possess the relic, what is our next step? What do we do with it?"

With determination, Sarah snatches the book and delves into its contents, devouring the text earnestly. As she absorbs the knowledge within, she breaks the silence with a resolute tone.

"The next step," she begins, "is to fully embrace the embodiment of Torquemada's inquisitors. We must don robes reminiscent of their sinister attire and perform a ritual of purification within the cellar, where they traditionally gathered."

Loren interjects with a hint of sarcasm, "So, to conquer the darkness, we must become one with it?" The room falls into silence, leaving his question unanswered.

Concerned, Hawthorne raises a practical query, "Where will we acquire these robes?" he asks.

Pritchard speaks up, his voice laced with uncertainty, "There should be some robes in one of the thirteen rooms within the cellar. But are we certain that this is the right path to take?"

Sarah locks eyes with Pritchard, and then addresses the entire group with unwavering conviction. "According to the writings, we must confront the darkness directly to vanquish it. We must place our trust in this process, Pritchard. It is our only opportunity to succeed."

Summoning every ounce of courage, the group ventures into the murky depths of the dimly lit cellar. The atmosphere is heavy with anticipation and a hint of trepidation.

Pritchard points towards a cluster of rooms on the opposite side of the cellar, his voice steady. "The robes are located in one of those rooms over there," he informs them, gesturing across the room, their path obstructed by the vat of acid. Hawthorne and Loren proceed to investigate, meticulously exploring each room until they discover the dusty black robes within the second one. They shake off the accumulated dust, readying themselves for the next step.

"Now what?" Loren queries, his tone filled with uncertainty.

"We must don these robes," Sarah responds firmly, slipping into hers. She consults the ancient text once again, scanning the room for a suitable means to mark the floor. "We require something more substantial than chalk," she muses, her gaze searching for a solution within the room's confines.

Pritchard directs their attention to another area of the room, his finger pointing towards the old workbench. "Look over there, by the old workbench. I believe I spotted a box of red paint cans," he suggests, his voice filled with a newfound determination. Intrigued, the group makes their way towards the workbench, finding a box of neglected paint cans covered in layers of dust.

Loren reaches out, his hand grasping one of the cans. "This will serve our purpose perfectly," he declares, pulling out the vibrant red paint can. The group gathers brushes, preparing to dip them into the paint, their eyes focused on the symbol that must be created as depicted in the ancient drawing.

As they commence their work, a palpable shift occurs within the cellar. An ethereal energy seems to awaken, causing the air to crackle with anticipation. It's as if the house itself senses the significance of their actions, its ancient spirit stirring in response.

Once the symbol is painstakingly complete, they step back to admire their handiwork. Hawthorne carefully compares it to the drawing, ensuring its accuracy and alignment. "Looks good to me. Let's just hope this works," Hawthorne says to no one in particular.

"We've done it. Now, let us ready ourselves for the ultimate stage of the ritual," Sarah declares with a newfound confidence.

"What's that?" Pritchard's curiosity prompts him to inquire.

Sarah turns her gaze back to the ancient text, her eyes scanning the page. "It says that each of us must assume a position around the symbol," she replies, her voice filled with conviction.

Loren's sudden exclamation draws their attention to the circle on the floor. "Look at the red paint," he points out. Their eyes widen as they witness the paint emitting a mysterious glow, casting an otherworldly reflection.

In that moment, a chilling gust of wind permeates the cellar, extinguishing the lamps one by one. The temperature in the cellar begins to drop quickly. Their breath escaping their lips, materializing into a hazy cloud that drifts momentarily in the cold atmosphere. From beneath the cover that conceals the vat of acid, a mist begins to rise, gradually taking shape. The mist coalesces, forming the spectral figure of the young girl Sarah and Hawthorne encountered earlier, her presence ominous and enigmatic.

The young female ghost hovers in the room, her ghostly form emitting an aura of foreboding. Her voice carries a sense of urgency and warning. "You are not yet strong enough to face Torquemada. He thrives on fear and despair, growing more powerful with each futile attempt to vanquish him. Time is running out. He is aware of your intentions. He is approaching. Run! Run!"

A second apparition materializes beside the young female ghost. It takes the form of Rachel Henry, her ethereal figure exuding an air of grace and tranquility. Hovering above the ground, she emanates an eerie yet comforting presence. Translucent and ethereal, her eyes reflect a blend of sorrow and optimism, a gentle soul bound by the mysteries of the afterlife.

Filled with a mixture of awe and curiosity, Sarah addresses the ghostly manifestation of Rachel Henry. "You're here," she whispers, her voice filled with wonder and a glimmer of recognition. Henry's spirit waves back and forth before she speaks.

"The girl speaks the truth. Torquemada's power is formidable, and the ritual in the ancient book alone is insufficient to vanquish his malevolent presence," the ghostly Rachel Henry imparts with a somber tone. "You must exit this cellar and seek additional guidance from the ancient text. The answer is in the text. You must all depart. Leave now, before it is too late." Her words hang in the air, a solemn warning urging them to take immediate action and find the necessary knowledge to combat the overwhelming force that lies within the house.

The group quickly leaves the cellar returning to the parlor.

CHAPTER 18

ONLY PRITCHARD TOOK a seat when the group arrived back at the parlor. "What do we do now? How can we become strong enough to defeat Torquemada?" Sarah asked, not really expecting a response but was surprised when Loren jumped in with a suggestion.

"I think we should go back to the library," Pritchard contributes. "There is nothing in this room except us and the ancient text. I don't recall seeing books in any of the other rooms."

Loren, echoing Pritchard's sentiment, adds with determination, "We must heed the guidance of the two spirits. We cannot afford to lose hope now. We need to continue delving into the depths of the ancient text. She said the answer is in the text. The library seems to hold the key to our escape from this house."

With a shared consensus, the group redirects their steps towards the library, propelled by the belief that within its walls lies the wisdom and secrets they seek. As they gather around a large wooden table in the ornate library, the ancient manuscript is carefully laid out before them. The room exudes an atmosphere of mystery, adorned with towering bookshelves filled with leather-bound tomes and dust-covered volumes. Flickering lamps cast eerie shadows across their faces, adding to the sense of anticipation.

Sarah gently turns the pages of the fragile manuscript, Loren and Hawthorne leaning in to observe. Together, they embark on the search for answers, their hearts filled with a glimmer of hope amidst the encroaching darkness that surrounds them.

Loren quickly found something in the text. "Look here, a passage about the ritual of purification. It speaks of a hidden chamber within the house—a place where Torquemada's evil is at its strongest."

"Purification?" Hawthorne asked frowning. "How do we cleanse ourselves in order to confront him?"

Prichard casually interjected, "Maybe we need to gather certain objects or artifacts to assist us. The text might uncover their purpose."

They meticulously combed through the manuscript, their gaze scanning the ancient words for any clue that could guide them to their next course of action. Suddenly, Sarah's finger came to a halt on a page, her eyes widening as a realization washed over her.

"I've found it! The text mentions an amulet of protection, a relic rumored to possess the power to ward off evil. It's said to be hidden within the depths of an ancient cemetery."

Loren is the first to comment. "Venturing into a cemetery? How? We can't get out of the house. It sounds treacherous."

"No, the text is actually referring to the graveyard on the other side of the house," Pritchard responded.

"The other side of the house? I didn't notice any graveyard there, just the cellar," Hawthorne said, expressing his frustration at the setback in their escape plan.

Unaware of Hawthorne's frustration, Pritchard continued, "This house holds numerous secrets from both its past and present. There are rumors that Torquemada and his demons, after torturing and killing their victims, buried them on the side of the house opposite to where we currently are. One of the previous owners sealed it off. To reach it, we'll have to break down the wall."

"And how are we going to do that?" Hawthorne asked, his voice filled with concern. "I used my gun in the upstairs bedroom, but that was made of sheetrock. It will be of little use against a wall made of stone."

The others exchanged worried glances, realizing the truth in Hawthorne's words. Their limited resources and weapons seemed insignificant in the face of the solid stone barrier that stood before them.

"Perhaps that coat of armor in the entrance hall will help," Loren suggested. They all quickly left the parlor heading towards the main entrance to the house.

As they arrived at the designated room, their eyes fell upon a majestic statue of a knight adorned in heavy armor, gripping a mace firmly in its hand. Hawthorne's gaze fixated on the weapon, a glimmer of determination shining in his eyes.

Without a moment's hesitation, he reached for the mace and tightened his grip around its handle. Testing its weight, he swung it experimentally, feeling the might and power coursing through his veins. The others watched, a mixture of awe and anticipation etched upon their faces.

"This should work," Hawthorne declared, his voice filled with a newfound confidence. "Okay, Pritchard, show us the way to the wall."

Pritchard assumed the role of the vanguard, his knife blade extended before him like a valiant knight's lance in a joust. Despite encountering a few erroneous turns along the convoluted corridors, he pressed on, leading the group. Their footsteps resonated in the unsettling stillness of the house, each sound magnified in the eerie atmosphere. At times, Pritchard's strides faltered, his path becoming uncertain, as if the very walls of the house conspired to bewilder his course.

Pritchard's eyes widened with triumph as he stumbled upon the correct wall. "It's on the other side of this wall," he exclaimed, relief washing over his face.

Hawthorne gestured for everyone to step back, giving him ample space to swing the mace. The survivors retreated a safe distance, their breaths held in anticipation. With a powerful swing, Hawthorne struck the wall with all his might, the impact sending chips of brick scattering through the air.

"This might take some time," Hawthorne remarked, his voice resolute. The groaning sound, originating from another part of the house, echoed through the corridors, adding an eerie soundtrack to their endeavors.

Pritchard, hearing the groans in the house intensify, and griping tightly to his butcher knife become very agitated. "We don't have much time. Keep swinging." After several minutes, larger chunks of the wall started to give way. Loren and Pritchard assisted in removing the debris. A foul odor permeated the air, catching everyone's attention.

"Sarah, give me my lighter," Hawthorne requested, his voice urgent and determined. Sarah swiftly handed him the lighter, and with a flick, the flame illuminated the dark void inside the damaged wall.

"What do you see?" Loren asked, his voice filled with anticipation and a hint of fear.

Hawthorne peered into the depths, his eyes narrowing as he tried to make sense of the scene before him. "Pritchard was right," he finally spoke, his voice tinged with disbelief. "There aren't any grave markers, but you can make out mounds of dirt indicating burials. I can't believe that when this place was brought from Spain here, the owner even brought the graveyard."

A shudder ran through the group as they absorbed the weight of Hawthorne's words. The thought of a relocated graveyard within the confines of the House on Haunted Hill sent chills down their spines.

"He didn't," Pritchard interjected, his voice filled with a mix of knowledge and unease. "My understanding was that one night, it just appeared. The owner was so frightened, he enclosed it with this large room to keep it contained."

As if responding to their discussion, the groaning sounds from other parts of the house grew louder, resonating through the air and chilling their bones. The growing cacophony added to the sense of dread and urgency that filled the group.

Hawthorne took the lead, cautiously climbing through the opening in the damaged wall, and one by one, the rest of the group followed suit. The flickering flame of Hawthorne's lighter cast a dim glow, illuminating their surroundings as they entered the mysterious burial ground.

Loren lit a candle, but it did not help. As the light danced across the area, Hawthorne surveyed the scene, his eyes widening at the eerie sight that unfolded before them. Mounds of earth stretched out in every direction, marking the resting places of the deceased. Shadows seemed to shift and dance amidst the tombstones, adding an ethereal quality to the atmosphere.

"Look, over there," Loren exclaimed, his voice filled with excitement. "It looks like a small mausoleum."

Hawthorne directed the light toward the dilapidated structure Loren had pointed out. Its stone walls bore the marks of time, and the entryway stood partially collapsed. Pritchard wore a puzzled expression on his face, his curiosity piqued.

"Why would Torquemada build a mausoleum?" Pritchard questioned, his voice tinged with intrigue.

"Maybe for his wife," Hawthorne speculated, his gaze still fixed on the weathered structure.

Pritchard's voice carried a note of correction. "Torquemada never entered wedlock. He vowed to lead a life of chastity." Hawthorne shrugged, acknowledging the discrepancy.

"It doesn't matter. Our priority is to gain access and see if the amulet is inside. "Sarah chimed in, her voice filled with determination. "Let's go."

The group advanced cautiously toward the decaying mausoleum; their footsteps muffled by the soft earth beneath them. With each step, their anticipation grew, their mission clear in their minds. They would find a way inside, uncover the secrets that lay within, and hopefully locate the amulet that held the key to their escape.

With trepidation, the group cautiously navigated the labyrinthine path that led them to the dilapidated mausoleum. Everywhere they looked, there was signs of burial plots. A sense of unease permeated the air, their every step accompanied by a growing sense of foreboding. The once-majestic structure now stood in disrepair, its wrought iron door barely clinging to its rusty hinges.

As they approached the mausoleum, their hearts raced with a mix of anticipation and fear. The ground beside the path seemed to stir, as if something restless lay beneath, struggling to break free from its confines. Unaware of the hidden turmoil beneath them, they pressed forward, their focus fixed on the chamber that awaited them within.

Loren, displaying both bravery and caution, stepped forward and pushed the creaking door open. A haunting creak pierced the silence as the dark chamber was revealed to the group. The flickering light from Hawthorne's lighter and Loren's candle barely penetrated the thick shadows that enveloped the interior. They found a torch and with the lighter, Hawthorne lit it. This greatly added to the illumination in the room.

A musty scent filled their nostrils, mingling with the dampness that clung to the air. The atmosphere within the mausoleum seemed heavy with secrets, and a palpable tension settled upon the survivors. They knew that whatever awaited them inside could hold the key to their ultimate fate.

As they hesitated at the threshold, their gazes met, their determination and resolve evident in their eyes. With a collective breath, they stepped forward, ready to face the darkness that awaited them within the chamber, their quest for the amulet guiding their every move. Little did they know the horrors that lay in wait, lurking in the shadows of Torquemada's mausoleum.

CHAPTER 19

WITH CAUTION, THE survivors stepped inside the mausoleum, the torch piercing through the suffocating darkness. Cobwebs clung to ancient coffins, their once ornate designs now faded and worn. The stale scent of decay filled the air, adding to the eerie atmosphere that enveloped them.

"It smells as bad in here as out there. Let's make this quick," Pritchard voiced with a trembling hint of fear. The sense of impending danger seemed to grow stronger with each passing moment.

Loren's eyes scanned the decaying caskets, his voice filled with a mix of curiosity and unease. "He built this mausoleum for his fellow inquisitors. Look, here is a tomb that was reserved for old Torquemada himself."

The group gathered around the tomb, the torch illuminating the faded engravings and ornate carvings that adorned its surface. Hawthorne's excited voice pierced through the tension-filled air, pointing to a nearby pedestal.

"Look! There, on that pedestal," he exclaimed, his voice filled with both excitement and anticipation. In the flickering flames of the torch, the group's gaze fell upon a radiant artifact—the amulet. Its surface bore intricate symbols etched with precision and ancient wisdom. The sight of it stirred a glimmer of hope within their hearts.

"This must be it. The amulet of protection," Sarah declared triumphantly, her voice brimming with confidence. "The text mentioned it would grant us strength in our battle against Torquemada."

A surge of determination surged through the group as they marveled at the artifact before them. They understood that this amulet held the key to their survival and the potential to overcome the dark forces that plagued them within the House on Haunted Hill.

With steady hands, Sarah reached out and delicately grasped the amulet, feeling a faint surge of energy course through her veins. The weight of their journey and the battles that lay ahead seemed to bear down upon them, but the amulet brought a glimmer of hope—a symbol of their resilience and a source of strength.

As the group gathered around Sarah to catch a glimpse of the amulet, an icy gust of wind swept through the chamber, causing the cracked walls to tremble. A chilling whisper filled the air, carried on the ethereal currents.

"Listen. Can you hear that?" Loren's voice trembled with a mixture of fear and urgency, drawing the attention of the group.

The whispers grew louder, their spectral voices filled with desperation and warning. "Get out! You need to get out! He's coming! He's coming! Run! Run!"

Startled by the haunting voices, Sarah tightened her grip on the amulet, her eyes wide with alarm. Without hesitation, she and the rest of the group made a frantic dash toward the mausoleum's entrance, their hearts pounding in their chests.

But as they reached the door, a chilling realization struck them—the entrance had slammed shut, sealing them within the sepulcher. The echoing sound reverberated through the chamber, amplifying their sense of entrapment.

Hawthorne, always quick to take action, hands the torch to Loren and stepped forward. With a determined expression on his face, he gripped the handle and pulled with all his might, but the aged barrier refused to yield. Frustration mingled with the growing frenzy of whispers that surrounded them.

Hawthorne's eyes flicked to his gun, a glimmer of resolve shining within them. He knew that desperate times called for desperate measures. Taking a step back, he aimed his weapon at the stubborn handle, preparing to take a shot.

"Everyone, take cover! Get behind those old coffins!" Hawthorne commanded, his voice cutting through the chaos. The group scrambled to find refuge, seeking shelter behind the worn and weathered coffins scattered throughout the mausoleum. With everyone safely hidden, Hawthorne took a final glance around to ensure their safety. Satisfied, he steadied his aim, his finger tightening around the trigger.

"Three, two, one." The gunshot shattered the eerie silence, its deafening blast reverberating through the mausoleum. Dust filled the air, causing cobwebs to sway in the aftermath of the explosion. The door handle disintegrated into several pieces, and the door itself swung open, revealing a path to potential escape.

A surge of relief flooded the group as the barrier gave way. They wasted no time, seizing the opportunity to flee from the haunting whispers that still echoed in their ears. With the amulet clutched tightly in Sarah's hand, they embarked on their frantic retreat, determined to outrun the encroaching darkness and the imminent arrival of Torquemada.

Their journey was far from over, but the gunshot had bought them a precious moment of respite—a chance to regroup, gather their strength, and forge ahead in their battle against the malevolent forces that plagued the House on Haunted Hill.

The group hastily fled from the chamber, their hearts pounding in their chests, only to be confronted by a macabre spectacle. Emerging from the mist-shrouded ground, the skeletons of Torquemada's victims clawed their way out of their earthen graves. The air filled with the eerie creaking and rattling of bones, a haunting symphony of suffering. Many of the skeletons bore twisted joints, remnants of the tortures they had endured in their final moments.

"Oh, my God," Sarah said as she looked for Hawthorne for protection. As the skeletal figures staggered toward the group, their hollow eye sockets fixed upon them, they repeated their warning in chilling whispers. A chill ran down their spines, and a sense of foreboding tightened its grip around their hearts.

Among the skeletal horde, one figure separated from the rest and approached Sarah and the group. Its voice, a raspy echo of the past, carried a desperate plea. "Get out... before it's too late." A second skeleton followed closely, its voice joining the chorus of warning. "Torquemada is coming with his men."

The group stood frozen, their faces etched with terror. Sarah's hands tightened around the amulet, its presence offering a faint glimmer of hope amidst the encroaching darkness. The weight of their mission and the impending danger bore down upon them, testing their resolve.

"We have to listen to them. We need to leave now!" Sarah's voice rang out, breaking the paralysis that held them captive.

Loren, his own fear palpable, nodded in agreement. "Agreed. We can't stay here any longer." With trembling steps, they began to back away, their eyes locked on the advancing legion of skeletons. Each movement they made, the skeletal figures grew more relentless, their whispers intensifying in urgency and desperation. The path ahead seemed fraught with peril, but they knew that staying meant certain doom.

Driven by fear and a glimmer of hope, the group retreated, their instincts urging them to escape the clutches of Torquemada and his impending arrival. They pressed on, their resolve tested by the relentless pursuit of the skeletal phantoms. Though their steps were heavy and their breaths ragged, they clung to the flickering hope that awaited them beyond the fog and the horrors that haunted the House on Haunted Hill.

CHAPTER 20

BACK IN THE parlor, the group found a temporary respite from the imminent threat of Torquemada and his men. Pritchard, his nerves frayed, sought solace in the embrace of a bottle, his trembling hand clutching a knife.

Sarah, her voice filled with determination, addressed the weary survivors. "We've obtained the amulet, but the spirits' warnings persist. Torquemada knows our intentions and is closing in on us. We have to attempt the ritual once more."

A collective weariness weighed upon the group, each one bearing the physical and emotional toll of their harrowing journey. Despite their fatigue and fear, they understood the urgency of their situation. Time was slipping away, and the longer they remained within the confines of the House on Haunted Hill, the stronger their formidable adversary grew.

Loren, his voice laced with a glimmer of hope amidst the darkness, posed an intriguing thought. "Is it just me, or do you feel that the ghosts in the cemetery may be trying to help us? Perhaps, in aiding us, we can also offer them some form of salvation."

His words hung in the air, resonating with the group. There was an unspoken realization that their fates were intertwined with those restless spirits, their shared struggle against Torquemada creating a bond of mutual reliance.

Sarah nodded, contemplating Loren's insight. "You might be right. Perhaps there is a way to break the cycle of torment for both the spirits and ourselves. We must find a way to end Torquemada's grip on this house and set them free."

A heavy silence settled over the room, the air thick with anticipation. Suddenly, the silence was shattered by a cacophony of eerie groans, followed by haunting laughter that sent chills down their spines. Prichard's hand tightened around his knife, his eyes scanning the room for any sign of danger. Sarah, determined and resolute, clutched the amulet with unwavering resolve.

Hawthorne and Loren exchanged bewildered glances, their hearts pounding in their chests. They had come face to face with the malevolent presence they had sought to vanquish. From the very floor itself, the ghostly figure of Torquemada materialized, his spectral form emanating an aura of malevolence. He was accompanied by a retinue of inquisitors, their ethereal presence adding to the chilling atmosphere.

Feeling the weight of their predicament, the four surviving individuals huddled around Sarah, seeking strength and protection in her presence. With a steady hand, she raised the amulet high, aiming it directly at Torquemada and his spectral entourage. The moment the radiant artifact came into view, the ghostly inquisitor recoiled, his ethereal form shrinking back. The other accompanying spirits mirrored his reaction, shielding their spectral faces from the power of the amulet.

A surge of hope coursed through the group as they witnessed the effect of the amulet's power on their supernatural adversaries. It was a temporary reprieve, but one that emboldened their determination to rid the House on Haunted Hill of Torquemada's malevolent influence.

In that tense moment, the boundaries between the living and the dead blurred as the survivors and the spirits locked gazes, each aware of the other's presence. It was a battle of wills, a struggle for freedom and redemption. The room crackled with an otherworldly energy, the clash between the living and the spectral realms reaching its climax.

Torquemada's voice resonated with authority, his words dripping with malevolence. "Each of you stands accused of heinous crimes, and the time for judgment and interrogation has come," he declared, a sinister smile curling on his ghostly visage. His eyes fixated on

Prichard, who cowered behind Loren, his trembling hand barely maintaining its grip on his knife.

"Pritchard, you are charged with the sin of debauchery, and I demand your plea," Torquemada intoned, relishing in the fear that gripped his victim. Terror consumed Prichard, his trembling hand seeking solace behind Loren's protective presence. The weight of the accusation pressed upon him, rendering him speechless and paralyzed by fear.

With a calculated shift of his gaze, Torquemada turned his attention towards Hawthorne. "And Hawthorne, you are accused of violating the Eighth Commandment, bearing false witness against your neighbor," he accused, a hint of confusion flickering across Hawthorne's face. His eyes darted towards the other survivors, seeking understanding and support.

Confusion mingled with defiance as Hawthorne retorted, "What are you talking about? I have done no such thing!"

Undeterred, Torquemada's attention then fell upon Sarah Owens, his accusing words piercing the air. "And you, Sarah Owens, stand accused of taking a life entrusted to your care. A weighty transgression that demands justice," he proclaimed, his voice filled with righteous indignation.

As the inquisition unfolded, the survivors found themselves trapped in Torquemada's merciless gaze. The ghostly figure then turned towards Frederick

Loren, his piercing eyes penetrating deep into Loren's soul, a silent accusation hanging in the air.

Torquemada's ethereal voice filled the room, growing more haunting and chilling as he addressed Frederick Loren. "And you, Frederick Loren, the greatest sinner of them all," he proclaimed, his words dripping with accusation. "You stand accused of the most heinous crimes, including the murder of your fourth wife and countless others. How do you plea?"

A mixture of shock and horror washed over the survivors as Torquemada unveiled the darkest secrets within Frederick Loren's past. The weight of the accusations hung heavily in the air, threatening to crush their hopes of escape.

Summoning her courage amidst the chaos, Sarah Owens stepped forward, her heart pounding with a mixture of bravery and terror. With a defiant determination shining in her eyes, she approached Torquemada, clutching the amulet tightly in her trembling hand. She refused to let fear consume her, ready to challenge the ghostly inquisitor's authority and protect her companions.

The room grew still as Sarah faced Torquemada, their eyes locked in a battle of wills. She could feel the immense power pulsating within the amulet, empowering her with the strength to confront this malevolent spirit.

With a resolute voice, Sarah boldly addressed Torquemada, "Your accusations may be filled with darkness, but we will not succumb to your torment. We stand united, ready to face whatever judgment you seek to impose. We will not be prisoners to your malevolence any longer."

As Torquemada recoiled in agony from Sarah's defiant act, and the presence of the amulet, he emited a piercing scream that echoed through the chamber, the other ghostly inquisitors, equally affected by the amulet's power, swiftly retreated, their spectral forms dissipating into the darkness like fading mist.

A palpable stillness settled upon the parlor, shrouding the survivors in an eerie calm. Hesitant breaths were drawn, each one carrying the weight of their experiences and the need for confession that lingered like a haunting presence. The temperature in the cellar began to rise.

CHAPTER 21

BREAKING THE HEAVY silence, Pritchard's voice emerged, trembling with sorrow and remorse. With hesitant steps, he moved forward, his eyes filled with tears that mirrored the pain in his soul. The weight of his guilt pressed upon him as he began to share his deepest secret, his voice filled with a mix of anguish and regret.

"What he said is true," Pritchard confessed, his voice choked with emotion. "You all already knew that I am an alcoholic, but there's something more... something I've kept buried deep within me for far too long."

As his words hung in the air, heavy with the weight of his past, Pritchard's trembling intensified. He took a moment to gather himself, his hands trembling as he continued to speak.

"Several years ago, before I ended up in the mental hospital, I took my only son out to dinner for his birthday," Pritchard began, his voice quivering. "His mother and I had divorced a long time ago due to my drinking. During that dinner, he confronted me about my alcoholism, pleading with me to change. But in my selfishness and denial, I laughed it off, dismissing his concerns."

A wave of guilt washed over Pritchard, tears streaming down his face as he struggled to find the right words. Sarah, moved by his confession, walked over, and embraced him, offering comfort in her compassionate presence.

"I don't know what happened that night, but as we drove home, I swerved into the path of an oncoming car," Pritchard's voice cracked, his pain palpable. "When I regained consciousness in the hospital, I learned that my son didn't make it. He died in the crash."

The room was consumed by an overwhelming sadness, the weight of Pritchard's confession reverberating through the walls. The depth of his guilt and the tragedy of his past laid bare for all to witness.

Pritchard wiped his tears with a trembling hand, his voice shaking with a mix of sorrow and remorse. "You would think that losing my son would have been enough to make me stop drinking, to change my ways. But instead, I sank even deeper into the bottle, drowning myself in the pain and self-destruction."

As Pritchard regained his composure, his confession hanging heavy in the air, Hawthorne stepped forward, a solemn expression etched on his face, ready to reveal his own hidden burden.

"Well, I guess it's good to unburden oneself of guilt by talking with a brother and sister about things that weigh so heavily on one's heart," Hawthorne began, his voice filled with a mix of remorse and vulnerability. The room remained hushed, everyone eager to hear his confession.

"I don't know how Torquemada found out about what I did when I was a police officer, and honestly, if I had the chance to go back and do it all over again, I would," Hawthorne admitted, his gaze fixed on the floor. Silence hung in the air as his words settled.

Years ago, I was the primary investigator assigned to the American River murder case," Hawthorne continued, his voice tinged with sorrow. Sarah interjected, her voice filled with shock and horror at the mention of the case.

"Oh, my God. The case where the murderer kidnapped those children, kept them as sex slaves, and when he grew tired of them, killed them and weighted their bodies in the river?" Sarah asked, her voice trembling with disbelief.

Hawthorne nodded solemnly. "That's the one," he confirmed. Loren, who had been away during that time, expressed his lack of knowledge about the case.

"I've never heard of it. I've been away," Loren stated, his tone filled with curiosity.

Hawthorne proceeded to provide details, painting a grim picture of the horrors that unfolded. "The first murder that we know of was discovered over fifteen years ago. A family went down to the river for a picnic and stumbled upon the submerged body of a young girl named Judy Turner. She was fourteen years old. We didn't know her identity at first, but with time and the help of an artist's sketch, we were able to identify her as a runaway from San Francisco."

Pritchard, intrigued by the story, expressed his interest. "I vaguely recall hearing about it on television. They interviewed her mother, who seemed rather detached from her daughter's loss."

Hawthorne corrected him, revealing the grim reality of Judy's home life. "No, her mother was a drug addict, which was one of the reasons Judy ran away. Her mother would bring men to their mobile home and engage in prostitution."

Sarah expressed her disgust, her voice filled with empathy for the young victim. "How repulsive," she whispered.

Hawthorne nodded in agreement. "Yes, the deterioration of family values was already apparent during that time," he said sadly.

Loren, eager to learn more, inquired about the number of victims. Hawthorne's expression turned somber as he shared the chilling truth. "Once we apprehended him, he admitted to twenty-one victims, but despite his cooperation, we were only able to recover the bodies of sixteen."

Curiosity led Loren to ask about the delay in capturing the murderer. Hawthorne's smile hinted at a shocking revelation. "The suspect was Gary Willis, a Criminal Justice Ph.D. student at UCLA. He would accompany various law enforcement agencies as part of his studies, even joining our homicide task force assigned to the American River murders to learn our techniques."

Loren returned the smile, understanding the twisted game that had unfolded. "So essentially, the police were unknowingly assisting him in perfecting his methods of evading capture."

Hawthorne nodded with a heavy heart. "Essentially, yes. He took great care to leave little to no forensic evidence, and the fact that he disposed of the bodies by submerging them made it even more challenging to gather evidence against him."

"How did you finally catch him?" Pritchard asked, his curiosity piqued.

"After seven long years of delivering devastating news to parents that their daughters would not be coming home, we finally had a breakthrough," Hawthorne began. "He attempted to kidnap a young girl as she was leaving school, but a vigilant crossing guard intervened. As he fled the scene, witnesses described him driving a dark blue Malibu. Through a statewide search, we narrowed down our suspects to six individuals, and once I interviewed him, I knew he was our man."

Pritchard leaned forward, eager to hear more. "So, what happened next?" he asked, anticipation in his voice.

"We obtained a search warrant for his car and house, but unfortunately, we found nothing incriminating,"

Hawthorne explained with a hint of frustration. "Gary simply laughed at us as we left empty-handed."

Loren interjected, voicing his confusion. "I fail to see how any of this relates to the accusations made by Torquemada," he remarked, seeking clarity.

Hawthorne continued, revealing the pivotal moment in the case. "While executing the search warrant in his bedroom, I secretly collected several strands of hair from his comb. Later, when we discovered the body of his next victim, I planted his hair under her fingernails."

Loren's face lit up with understanding. "So essentially, you framed him," he stated, recognizing the clever tactic used by Hawthorne.

Hawthorne nodded, acknowledging the truth of Loren's statement. "When a witness spotted his car at the scene of another attempted kidnapping, we obtained another search warrant and collected hair fibers. The rest, as you can imagine, is history. During his interrogation, he smirked at me, claiming he knew we had set him up, which ultimately proved to be his downfall."

Curiosity filled Sarah's eyes as she posed a question. "What mistake did he make?"

"He made a crucial mistake," Hawthorne replied with a sense of satisfaction. "He stated that we could never find any hair on any of his victims because he always washed them before dumping them in the river. However, his slip-up was caught on tape.

Eventually, he was convicted and sentenced to death, but he ended up taking his own life in prison."

Sarah expressed her satisfaction with the outcome. "So he got what he deserved," she said, a hint of relief in her voice.

Pritchard echoed her sentiment. "I agree," he chimed in, his voice filled with a mix of justice and closure.

Hawthorne acknowledged their support, feeling a weight lift off his shoulders as he concluded his confession. "Nevertheless, this is what our tormentor is alluding to," he said, his tone a mixture of acceptance and relief.

Sarah flips over an ancient textbook, her gaze shifting to everyone in the room. "I've carried this guilt for five years," she admitted. "If we manage to escape this house, I will turn myself in to the police once I ensure my mother is taken care of." Tears well up in her eyes and she holds onto the table addressing the group.

"As I told you, I work at County General, originally assigned to the terminal illness unit. I've been there for almost six years now. Despite trying to maintain a professional distance and not getting attached to patients, I had formed a deep bond with one of them. Angie was nearing her ninety-fourth birthday, with no family or friends. She felt immense suffering and questioned why she was still alive and enduring such pain." Sarah breaks down, and Hawthorn approaches her, offering a comforting hug.

"Angie had Stage IV pancreatic cancer, causing excruciating pain. Despite multiple unsuccessful chemo treatments, her condition worsened. We were authorized to administer morphine for her pain, but she still writhed in agony. She became like a grandmother to me. So, I took morphine from another patient who didn't really require it and intentionally overdosed Angie, releasing her from further suffering. She passed away shortly afterward, with me by her side, holding her hand. I knew I wouldn't get caught since she was under a doctor's care, and her prognosis was only a few days at most."

Silent fills the room as Sarah embraces Hawthorne, and Pritchard pours himself another glass of wine. The group forms a solemn circle, their faces reflecting compassion, remorse, and an understanding of human fallibility.

"Alright then. I guess we should proceed back to the cellar one last time and start the ritual," Loren said moving towards that location.

"Wait a minute, Loren," Hawthorne interjected, causing everyone's gaze to shift towards him. "Torquemada appeared to have a heightened interest in you," he continued, his words laden with intrigue and concern.

Loren cleared his throat, steeling himself for what he was about to reveal. "Very well then. Where should I begin? Oh, how about the murder of my wife?"

Pritchard interjected, recounting their earlier conversation. "He approached me to rent this place, and I warned him about its haunted reputation and the potential for tragedy, but he insisted."

"I didn't hear you voicing any complaints when I offered you a substantial sum of money for the property," Loren responded combatively. Pritchard scoffed and took a sip of his wine.

"After acquiring the keys to this place, I enlisted a few trusted employees from my company to help set up Halloween decorations inside the house and invited my guests. Most of them didn't know each other, just like you. But I made sure that Annabelle's lover would be present."

"Good Lord, Loren. If you planned on killing them, it would be premeditated murder," Hawthorne pointed out, his voice filled with shock and disbelief.

Loren glanced at him, his defensive stance evident. "Yes, it was, and I served a twenty-year sentence for it," he replied firmly.

Hawthorne's curiosity peaked. "I didn't follow your trial closely, but did you confess to killing both of them?" he inquired.

Loren nodded, a somber expression crossing his face. "Yes, I did admit to it. However, during the trial, I presented evidence that I acted in self-defense when it came to shooting my wife's lover. You see, the jury learned about their conspiracy to kill me that very night in this house. Annabelle's lover pursued me downstairs with a handgun. Thankfully, I heard him on the cellar stairs, and, in a desperate moment, I turned off the lights and fired in self-defense before he could harm me."

"Then you dragged his body over to the vat of acid and later used his skeleton to lure your wife to the pit," Pritchard interjected, his tone filled with accusation. Loren smiled and raised an eyebrow.

"No, Mr. Pritchard. It wasn't anything so grotesque," Loren calmly responded. "I had already prepared a skeleton in the cellar as part of my Halloween party decorations. It was purely for entertainment purposes. However, when my 'beloved' wife descended the stairs, calling out for her lover, I decided to incorporate the skeleton into the scene for dramatic effect."

"So, you frightened her to death?" Sarah asked, her voice filled with shock and disbelief.

"No, I'm afraid the acid did that," he replied with a sinister grin on his face.

Loren's expression grew even darker as he continued, his voice filled with malice. "Sadly, our marriage, my fourth and her third, had reached its bitter end. I wanted a divorce, but she vehemently refused," he explained.

Hawthorne, intrigued by the unfolding tale, inquired, "Why did she resist the divorce?"

A chilling smile played upon Loren's lips as he responded, "Ah, because a divorce would entitle her to only a portion of my estate. However, if something were to happen to me, especially in an accident, she would not only inherit the estate but also collect the substantial payout from my life insurance policy, thanks to its double indemnity clause. Fate had a way of revealing her true nature to me, as I discovered her involvement in a sordid affair with a psychiatrist, who was complicit in her sinister scheme. It was then that I hatched a plan to host a party for her right here, in this very house."

"When he approached me about renting this place, I warned him that it was haunted, and that people would meet their demise. But he insisted," Pritchard reiterated, obviously drunk. A heavy silence descended upon the room, the weight of Loren's words lingering in the air.

In the midst of the tense atmosphere, Sarah's eyes widened as she carefully flipped over the ancient text she had been scanning. With a sense of urgency, she turned to face the group, instantly capturing their attention. "Wait! I think I've stumbled upon something significant. The confessions we just made... they hold a deeper meaning according to this text," she exclaimed.

Curiosity roused, Hawthorne leaned forward, asking, "What do you mean, Sarah? What does the text say?"

Sarah took a moment to gather her thoughts before continuing, "It states that those who form the sacred circle must undergo a purification of their sins. In other words, a confession. The room fell into a hushed silence as Hawthorne, Pritchard, and Loren exchanged puzzled glances.

Sarah's voice grew stronger as she elaborated, "Think about it. Each confession we've heard represents a sin committed by each of us. By acknowledging and confessing these sins, we've taken the first step towards purging ourselves of guilt and darkness. It's a process of purification. Now, we must delve deeper into the ritual and gather the strength to confront Torquemada."

Sarah's words settles on the other three. Loren has a guilty look on his face not noticed by the others. Sarah returns to reading the text.

Sarah's voice trembled with a mix of urgency and determination as she shared the revelation from the ancient text. "It says here that Torquemada draws his power from our sins and weaknesses. By confronting our past actions, by acknowledging and confessing them, we diminish his hold on us and on this house. It is through our strength, both individually and as a group, that we can complete the ritual and bring an end to Torquemada's reign."

Hawthorne, sensing the gravity of the situation, spoke up. "Well then," he said with resolve. "I guess it is time to return to the cellar." Reluctantly, the rest of the group nodded in agreement, recognizing the necessity of facing the darkness that awaited them below.

CHAPTER 22

THEY MADE THEIR way back to the dimly lit cellar. Loren's gaze briefly falls upon the closed vat of acid before averting his eyes. As a group, they approach the painted circle they had created earlier. Sarah delicately places the sacred amulet around her neck.

Assuming her position at the forefront, Sarah prepares herself to lead the group in the ancient chant. An unsettling symphony of groans and screams begins to crescendo, seeping into the very essence of the house's walls.

"We must each take our place around the circle once again," Sarah instructs. The others follow her guidance, assuming their positions as the circle begins to radiate a faint glow, its center pulsating. They exchange glances, a mix of anticipation and determination reflected in their eyes.

"Everything is going according to plan. Let us continue," Hawthorne affirms.

Sarah recites the chant precisely as written in the text.

"In the depths of darkness, under Torquemada's reign,

We gather strength to break his binding chain.

With unified spirits, our voices entwined,

We banish evil, leaving no trace behind.

Within this sacred circle, we stand firm and true,

Undoing Torquemada's power, it's what we shall do.

Through ancient words, our plea is proclaimed.

Free this realm from his malevolent claim.

By the brilliance of light and the warmth of love's embrace.

We cast away Torquemada, nevermore to face.

With each resounding chant, his grip shall sever, Invoking the radiance that banishes forever.

Torquemada, your time has come to cease.

In this sacred rite, we find our release.

Be gone, be gone, depart this realm in peace.

In the name of all that's good, our strength will increase.

With unwavering faith, we reclaim this dwelling.

Erasing Torquemada's darkness, all compelling.

By our will and ancient rites, we command.

The spirit of Torquemada, leave this land."

The cellar chamber fills with a cacophony of bangs, groans, and screams. The lamps flicker erratically, casting eerie shadows across the room. The door covering the vat of acid creaks open of its own accord. Thirteen doors swing open abruptly and then slam shut with a resounding force.

From the cemetery, the once-buried souls of Torquemada's tormented victims slowly rise, breaking free from their dirt-covered graves. Hovering above the ground, their ghostly figures exude an eerie presence, their eyes reflecting a haunting blend of anguish and resolve. Drawn by an invisible force, they are inexorably drawn towards the cellar.

Simultaneously, the ghostly apparition of Torquemada himself lets out a blood-curdling scream as he emerges from his painted prison on the library wall. Following closely behind him are his loyal inquisitors, their spectral forms trailing behind. They depart from the confines of the bedroom, passing through the wall and venturing into the dimly lit hallway.

As Sarah persists in her chant, the intensity of the lamps flickering and the doors slamming amplifies with an alarming ferocity. In the midst of this chaos, Torquemada, accompanied by his malevolent henchmen, descends from the ceiling. Their cold, piercing gazes fixate upon Sarah and the rest of the group. Sarah abruptly halts her incantation, a scream escaping her lips. The sudden intrusion leaves the group stunned, their belief in the protective power of the amulet shattered.

With swift and calculated movements, Torquemada and his inquisitors charge towards the sacred circle, catching the group off guard. In a disheartening twist, the forces of darkness breach their defenses. Torquemada's icy grip wraps around Loren, wrenching him away from the safety of the circle, forcibly dragging him to a distant corner of the cellar.

In an instant, the room undergoes a horrifying transformation, morphing into a grotesque torture chamber. Helplessly, the group watches as Loren is stretched out upon a menacing rack, his body vulnerable to the sadistic whims of Torquemada and his minions.

Loren finds himself beneath the haunting presence of Torquemada's ghostly spirits, their ethereal forms floating ominously above him. With a voice filled with accusation, Torquemada addresses Loren, invoking a chilling question, "Frederick Loren, you stand accused of murder. How do you plead?"

Sarah, unable to bear the torment inflicted upon Loren, shouts defiantly, "He's already confused! Leave us be!"

Torquemada's gaze shifts from Sarah to Loren, his spectral eyes piercing into the depths of his soul. "Did he now?" he sneers. With a bony finger extended, Torquemada directs attention to the ceiling. Through a macabre reenactment, the group witnesses horrifying scenes.

The first shows Loren pushing Jeannie Manning down the stairs, leading to her untimely demise. The next reenactment portrays Loren cornering Stacey, forcing her into a pit, before sealing their fate by immersing their bodies in the vat of acid.

Denial twists Loren's face, his features contorted in anguish as the weight of the revealed truth engulfs him. As the inquisitors tighten the rack, tormenting him with searing pain, Frederick Loren vehemently protests, his voice echoing through the chamber, "No! It's not true! Those images, they are twisted lies!"

Torquemada and his inquisitors exchange a knowing glance, the malevolence in their eyes escalating. With an insidious smile, they tighten the rack even further, amplifying Loren's suffering to unbearable levels.

"Deny it no longer, Frederick Loren," Torquemada responds with cruel satisfaction. "The rack shall extract the truth from your very bones."

As grimaces contort his face and tears well up in his eyes, Loren finally succumbs to the weight of his guilt. His voice trembles as he confesses, "Alright, alright! I admit it! It's all true!" The inquisitors of Torquemada, sensing his vulnerability, ease the pressure on the rack, allowing him to speak.

Loren's voice quivers with anguish as he continues, "I killed Jeannie Manning... and Stacey too. I couldn't bear their betrayal. I discovered that Stacey, who possessed the ability to forge my signature during my time in prison, conspired with Ms. Manning to alter my trust. They planned for me to meet my demise in this house, a result of a staged accident down those very stairs, while she would inherit everything."

A triumphant smirk creeps across Torquemada's face, relishing in his twisted satisfaction. His cold gaze peers down upon Loren with indifferently cruel eyes. Raising his hand, he commands his inquisitors to carry out his dreadful sentence. "The time for redemption has passed, Frederick Loren. Your confession may be acknowledged, but your punishment remains."

Without mercy, Torquemada's inquisitors begin to turn the rack, their determination unwavering. The metallic creaking reverberates throughout the chamber as Loren's body is subjected to excruciating torment. His screams grow louder and more agonizing.

"No! I beg you, please have mercy!" Loren pleads in desperation.

Sarah's eyes widen in horror, a scream of terror escaping her lips. Amidst the chaos, Hawthorne's voice cuts through the anguish, commanding their attention. "Sarah, begin the chant once more! Now that we've confessed, we are purified within the circle," Hawthorne implores. "Our unity will shatter the darkness that consumes us!"

Sarah, shaken but resolute, summons her courage. Taking a deep breath, she quivers yet determinedly recites the chant once more, her voice infused with a newfound strength.

"In the depths of darkness, our spirits rise.

With purity and hope, evil meets its demise.

Together we stand, united we prevail.

Break the chains of torment, let goodness unveil...

The remaining members of the group, their determination etched upon their faces, unite their voices in the resounding chant. Their words intertwine, creating a surge of energy that floods the chamber. Torquemada and his inquisitors, caught off guard, panic and begin to frantically circle the room, their groans and screams filling the air. Gradually, as the energy intensifies, their ghostly forms start to fade away.

Sarah's voice rises above the rest, infused with unwavering resolve. The weight of their confessions and the purity of their intentions fuel their collective will to banish Torquemada and his reign of terror. With each verse, the oppressive atmosphere that once suffocated the chamber begins to dissipate. The room quakes as the torture chamber vanishes, along with the body of Loren. The cellar returns to its normal shape, its haunting presence lifted.

Suddenly, a blinding burst of radiant energy erupts, filling the space with its brilliance. The ghosts of Torquemada's victims materialize, their ethereal figures merging their energy with the group of chanters. They dart around Torquemada and his men, who swing futilely at them, devoid of power or influence.

Torquemada and his inquisitors recoil, their forms weakening and dissipating under the overwhelming assault of pure, untainted power. The room returns to its usual state, save for the lingering presence of

Torquemada's victims' ghostly figures, still circling the ceiling. Their spectral presence serves as a reminder of the triumph of light over darkness, and the group breathes a collective sigh of relief as the oppressive grip of Torquemada's reign is finally shattered.

CHAPTER 23

PRITCHARD OPENS HIS eyes. "Is it over?"

Hawthorne and Sarah stare in awe at the circling child spirits. Just then, the earlier young female ghost that had visited Sarah and Hawthorne, descends from the ceiling and hovers over the three."Thank you. We are now free." As she says this, the other spirits begin to leave going through the ceiling. The young girl spirits rise through the roof towards heaven.

Sarah goes into Hawthorn's arms. The glowing circle dims and then is extinguished.

As the spirits continue circling overhead leaving the house, they repeat the words over and over. "Thank you. Thank you. Thank you."

Hawthorne was the first of the trio to awaken in the parlor, greeted by the sight of the clock displaying 9:45 A.M., a mere 15 minutes before the house was scheduled to open. Filled with curiosity, he approached the entrance door and, to his surprise, discovered it unlocked. Without hesitation, he hurried back to Sarah and Pritchard.

"Sarah, Pritchard. The house is already open. We can leave," Hawthorne informed them.

"But Loren said it wouldn't open until 10 A.M.," Sarah voiced her confusion.

"I suppose that the liberation of those tormented souls and the banishment of Torquemada broke whatever spell or power he had over this place," Hawthorne speculated.

"Let's not dwell on it, but rather seize this opportunity to get the hell out of here," an excited Pritchard exclaimed. The three of them stepped outside and witnessed three black limousines ascending the hill, slowly approaching the house. Shaken but triumphant from their collective ordeal, they exchanged glances, their newfound friendship forged through the harrowing experience.

The limousines parked neatly in a row, their drivers standing beside the open doors, donning dark suits and impassive expressions. "I can already tell you that the police won't believe a word of what we tell them," Hawthorne remarked.

"I hadn't considered that. Six people lost their lives tonight, and yet, we lack concrete evidence to support our story," Sarah replied with a hint of concern.

"One thing is certain, though. The ghosts won't utter a single word. They will patiently await the arrival of their next victims," Pritchard chimed in, his tone serious.

Hawthorne contemplated the situation and suggested, "I believe we should have these limo drivers take us to the police department. It is their duty to determine the veracity of our account, whether we are telling the truth or merely a group of deranged individuals in need of psychiatric care."

"You just had to bring that up, didn't you?" Pritchard responded with a smile on his face, prompting a short burst of laughter from Sarah and Hawthorne.

Sarah, Hawthorne, and Pritchard find themselves seated in separate limousines, seeking solace within the luxurious interiors after the nightmarish ordeal they had endured. As the limousines move along, each driver hands their respective passenger a sealed envelope, adding a touch of intrigue to the already bewildering situation.

Curiosity piqued, Sarah's limo driver extends the envelope towards her. "What's this?" she inquires.

"It's from Frederick Loren. He wanted me to inform you that it is a token of his gratitude for your bravery and survival," the driver explains.

Meanwhile, Hawthorne finds himself lost in contemplation of the evening's events when his driver hands him a package. "Mr. Loren instructed me to give you this envelope as soon as I picked you up," the driver shares.

Hawthorne opens the package, his astonishment growing as he realizes its contents. "Wait... it's... it's a hundred thousand dollars," he exclaims, caught off guard by the unexpected generosity.

In a parallel turn of events, Pritchard also discovers the substantial sum of $100,000 within the envelope handed to him. Overwhelmed by the gesture, he gazes at the driver, seeking an explanation. "But why?" he wonders aloud.

The driver, wearing a warm smile, responds, "It's Mr. Loren's final gesture, a way to honor those who faced their fears and emerged victorious."

Intrigued by the contents of her envelope, Sarah finally musters the courage to open it. As she does, her eyes widen in astonishment at the substantial amount enclosed. However, her surprise doesn't end there. She discovers a second small envelope within the package, prompting her to open it as well. The contents within the second envelope further captivate her attention.

With Sarah's limousine leading the way, she instructs her driver to pull over and signals for the other drivers to do the same. The group, eager to uncover the significance of their unexpected rewards, gathers outside the vehicles, ready to unveil the mysteries concealed within the envelopes.

Hawthorne and Pritchard step out of their limousine, holding their envelopes tightly, and join Sarah, who wears a joyful smile on her face. Their excitement is palpable as they gather together.

Hawthorne, unable to contain his curiosity, asks eagerly, "What's inside? Did you also receive $100,000?"

Sarah's eyes sparkle with delight. "Yes, I did, but there's more. I have a legal document here." She pauses, savoring the moment before revealing the astonishing news. "We have been named the beneficiaries of Frederick Loren's estate. Each of us will receive an equal share of 50%."

Hawthorne's jaw drops in disbelief, his mind racing to comprehend the magnitude of their unexpected fortune. "Loren's estate... shared between us?" he utters, a mixture of shock and gratitude coloring his words.

Pritchard, holding his envelope, interjects with a hint of humor in his voice. "Well, I did receive $100,000, but it seems I won't be sharing in Loren's grand estate after all."

As if on cue, Pritchard's limo driver approaches them with a smile, bearing intriguing news. "Sir, the house on Haunted Hill now belongs to you. Mr. Loren, in his wisdom, decided to pass it on to the one who dared to expose its secrets and showed immense bravery by entering it three times."

Pritchard's expression undergoes a transformation, a mix of surprise and contemplation. "Then I shall tear it down, rid the world of its cursed legacy once and for all, and claim what the land is worth."

The three friends erupt into laughter, their joyous spirits intertwining as they embrace, united in their newfound wealth and purpose. After sharing a moment of celebration, they return to their respective limousines and drive down the hill, unaware of the events unfolding inside the house.

From within the structure, screams and groans continue to emanate, but Rachel Henry, Madame Redzepova, Jonathan Riley, Jeannie Manning, Stacey, and Frederick Loren's ghostly apparitions peer through the windows, wondering how long it will be before others dare to enter the House on Haunted Hill once more.

EPILOGUE

I extend my heartfelt gratitude for embarking on this literary journey through my contemporary novel, which draws inspiration from the timeless classic, "House on Haunted Hill." I am honored to pay tribute to the brilliant cast including Vincent Price, Carol Ohmart, Richard Long, Alan Marshal, Carolyn Craig, Elisha Cook Jr., and Julie Mitchum, as well as the talented screenwriter Robb White III.

As we delve into the narrative, it is fascinating to uncover the behind-the-scenes details of the film's production. The exterior shots of the house were filmed at the historic Ennis House in Los Feliz, California, an architectural masterpiece designed by Frank Lloyd Wright in 1924. Meanwhile, the interior of the house was meticulously recreated on sound stages, blending various styles, notably the Victorian era with its gas chandeliers and sconces from the 1890s.

Notably, the film's theatrical trailer advertised it as "The House on Haunted Hill," while all other promotional materials and the film itself carried the simpler title of "House on Haunted Hill." An ingenious promotional gimmick known as "Emergo" was employed during the movie's original release. In select theaters, an elaborate pulley system would suspend a plastic skeleton, soaring over the audience during a climactic scene, adding an extra layer of immersive terror.

The film's success owes much to the creativity of its director, William Castle, and his penchant for innovative marketing strategies. The impact of "House on Haunted Hill" did not go unnoticed, capturing the attention of none other than Alfred Hitchcock himself. Inspired by the film's achievements on a modest budget, Hitchcock went on to create his own iconic low-budget horror masterpiece, "Psycho," in 1960. Castle, an ardent Hitchcock fan, sought to emulate the master filmmaker's style in subsequent works like "Homicidal" in 1961.

Throughout the pages of my novel, my intent was to capture the essence of the original film, which has left an indelible mark on me. Even today, its influence remains potent, standing alongside Stephen King's "Rose Red" as a benchmark for haunted house movies.

Reflecting on the dedication section of this novel, I am reminded of the profound impact that "House on Haunted Hill" continues to exert on me. I sincerely hope that my writing has allowed you to experience the same sense of wonder, horror, and exhilaration that enthralled me within the chilling halls of the House on Haunted Hill.

It is worth noting that other screenwriters have revisited this compelling theme, resulting in subsequent films. The first among them was the 1999 release of "House on Haunted Hill," directed by William Malone and featuring a talented cast including Geoffrey Rush, Famke Janssen, Taye Diggs, Ali Larter, Bridgette Wilson, Peter Gallagher, and Chris Kattan.

This iteration follows a group of strangers invited to a party at an abandoned insane asylum, where they are offered a hefty sum of money if they can survive the night. It introduced advancements in special effects, which were skillfully incorporated throughout the film.

In 2007, the theme resurfaced in "Return to the House on Haunted Hill," directed by Victor Garcia and written by William Massa. The film stars Amanda Righetti, Tom Riley, Cerina Vincent, and Erik Palladino, as it explores the story of Ariel Wolfe, the younger sister of a character from the previous film. Forced to search for a mysterious idol within an abandoned and haunted psychiatric asylum, this installment adds a slight twist to the narrative. However, it bypassed theatrical release, arriving directly on DVD, Blu-ray, and HD DVD formats on October 16, 2007.

With pride, I present this novel as an unprecedented foray into the House on Haunted Hill, unveiling its mysteries two decades later since the film first appeared on the screen. Whether readers are acquainted with the original film or not, I have ensured ample context is provided.

Respecting the very essence of the original story, I have set my tale against the backdrop of the iconic house itself.

Perhaps, in the future, these very pages will grace the silver screen, captivating audiences with their chilling allure, evoking cherished memories for those who, as ten-year-old's, were terrorized by a film they would never forget.

FINAL TRIBUTE

Vincent Price
Frederick Loren

Carol Ohmart
Annabelle Loren

Richard Long
Lance Schroeder

Carolyn Craig
Nora Manning

Elisha Cook Jr.
Watson Pritchard

Alan Marshal
Dr. David Trent

Julie Mitchum
Ruth Bridgers

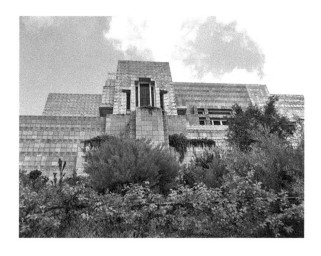

Ennis House, Los Angeles, California

In 1959 the exterior was featured in
House on Haunted Hill starring Vincent Price.